ZACKTASTIC

COURTNEY SHEINMEL

Book One

PUBLISHED BY SLEEPING BEAR PRESS

Sleeping Bear Press™

2395 South Huron Parkway, Suite 200, Ann Arbor, MI 48104
www.sleepingbearpress.com
© Sleeping Bear Press

Printed and bound in the United States.
10 9 8 7 6 5 4 3 2 1

Library of Congress Cataloging-in-Publication Data
Sheinmel, Courtney.
Zacktastic / written by Courtney Sheinmel.
pages cm
Summary: On his tenth birthday, Zack learns from his uncle that he is descended from
a long line of genies and before he has a chance to process this information, he is whisked
through a bottle portal and sent on his first assignment.
ISBN 978-1-58536-934-8 (hardcover) – ISBN 978-1-58536-935-5 (paperback)
[1. Genies–Fiction. 2. Wishes–Fiction. 3. Brothers and
sisters–Fiction. 4. Twins–Fiction. 5. Uncles–Fiction.
6. Birthdays–Fiction.] I. Title.
PZ7.S54124Zac 2015
[Fic]–dc23
2015003508

For Nicki, Andrew, and of course Zach

1

A Day in the Life

When you're interviewing yourself in the bathroom mirror, a fist under your chin makes the perfect microphone.

I pat my hair down so it falls around my head like a helmet. That's the way Drew Listerman, the reporter on the Channel 7 news, wears his hair. Every weekend he hosts a special called *A Day in the Life*, where he follows celebrities around and viewers get to see what a typical day is like for them.

I tuck a fallen strand behind my left ear, furrow my brows to make a wrinkle just above the bridge of my nose, and round my shoulders like Drew Listerman.

And I'm on.

"Good evening, ladies and gentleman. Today we're celebrating a day in the life of Zachary Cooley. Maybe you saw his picture in the newspaper on the day he stomped out a bunch of smoldering cigarette butts in the Pinemont Woods, preventing what surely would have been Pennsylvania's most massive forest fire. Or perhaps you heard his name mentioned on the radio the morning he spotted a woman walking on the railroad tracks and got her to safety just moments before a speeding train whipped by. Certainly you saw the story on the evening news about the time Zack rappelled out of a helicopter and rescued a man swimming in the ocean below. Seconds later a school of great white sharks was spotted off the coast. Young Zack is credited with saving hundreds–no, thousands!–of lives. Please join me in welcoming birthday boy Zachary

Noah Cooley, a real-life superhero!"

I imagine viewers all over the country and around the world clapping and cheering and waiting to see me, and I run a hand through my hair so it's back in my regular style, on the longish side and messed up like I just went for a superfast ride in a convertible, top down. Then I hold my fist out toward my reflection.

"Well, first off, Drew, I don't know that I'd call myself a superhero." I pause for a second, and in my head a few thousand voices talk back to their TVs: *What, Zack?! Of course you are!* "But second of all, I'm here to save even more lives with a special message. And that message is: Listen to your fears."

"I thought the only thing to fear is fear itself," Drew says.

"Sorry, Drew," I say. "But you—and Franklin Delano Roosevelt—are sadly mistaken. There are more things to fear than you could possibly count."

"Such as?"

"Such as: Aren't you afraid to walk too close to the edge of a roof?"

I can see Drew nodding. Of course he is.

"You're afraid because you could fall off," I tell him. "And I bet you're afraid to climb into the lions' cage at the zoo because you know they can eat you. These are good fears to have because they stop you from doing something that could hurt you–or even kill you. Having fears saves lives."

"I've never thought of it that way before," Drew Listerman says. "But it's certainly an important message you're spreading. In fact, it's practically a birthday present to us all. When really, we should be showering *you* with presents–especially on a birthday this significant. Tell me, how does it feel to hit double digits?"

"It's a funny thing," I say. "When I woke up this morning, something felt different." I peer a bit closer into the mirror–closer into the camera. "You ever get the feeling that something is changing in your life, that you're in for something particularly extraordinary?"

As I say it I feel a tingle run down my spine, like it's true. Like I'm onto something. Like there actually are people out there, right now, watching me, and something big is going to happen right before their eyes.

And then.

"BOO!" Quinn yells.

"Ahh!" I stumble backward. "You almost gave me a heart attack!" I shout at my sister. "What are you doing in here anyway?"

The bathroom door had been closed. I'm sure of it. I hadn't locked it, but that's because I broke all the locks in our house a couple of months ago. Do you know how many people die each year because they lock themselves into their bedrooms or bathrooms, and a fire starts up, and no one can get to them in time to save them?

Okay, I don't know, either. But I bet a lot of people do.

Mom was pretty mad about all the broken locks. But it was for her own good. Quinn's, too. Dad once told me that the three of us—Mom, Quinn, and I—were the most important people in his life, and he'd do anything to protect us. After what happened to him, it's up to me to make sure no one in my family ever gets hurt again. That's what Dad would want me to do.

But never mind that, because right now there's no fire, not even the thinnest curlicue of smoke. And in the absence of a fire, we all know that a closed door means don't come in.

Not that Quinn cares. She's bent in half, laughing. She laughs in a really squeaky, finger-nails-on-the-chalkboard, little-hairs-on-your-arms-standing-up kind of way: *Hee-eee-eee-EEEEEE. Hee-eee-eee-EEEEEE.* Her laugh is just as embarrassing as my little interview. Even worse, actually, because my interview was supposed to be private. But Quinn laughs that way all the time in public. She can't help herself.

Quinn stands straight and makes a big production out of trying to catch her breath, like it was just sooooo funny, she might not ever be able to breathe again. "You should've"–*pant, eeeeee, pant*–"seen yourself." *Pant, pant.* "Only a Grade A official nut job would talk to himself in the mirror." She pauses to take one long, deep gulp of a breath.

"I've seen *you* talk to yourself in the mirror," I tell her. And then I mimic her in a high-pitched voice: "Quinn, your hair looks so good. Quinn, I love your nail polish."

"At least I'm not pretending to be brave to my *imaginary* friends, when the truth is you're scared of everything. Are you sure you're turning ten today? Because you're acting like a baby."

"Babies aren't scared, because they don't know any better," I say. "It's actually a sign of maturity to be scared."

"Whatever. It's no wonder you don't have any friends."

"I do so have friends," I tell her.

"Yeah, right."

"And besides, I–"

"I can't wait to hear this," Quinn interrupts.

If she can't wait, she should be quiet and listen. "I'd rather have *no* friends than have *your* friends. Your friends are so . . . are so . . ."

Quinn is standing there with her hands on her hips, shaking her head at me like she's the older sister. But really we're twins, and if you want to get specific about it, *I'm* the older one. Seven minutes older. Seven minutes that I packed a lot of wisdom into.

"Your friends are so *slame*," I say.

"Oh, you got me this time," Quinn says. But she rolls her eyes so I know she doesn't mean it. "I'm so hurt by one of your dumb words that's not even a real word."

"It is a word," I insist. "*Slame*. Adjective. The same amount of lame as Quinn."

One day I'm going to write a dictionary of

all the words that should be part of the English language. *Slame* is one of my best words yet.

"Whatevs," she says. She flips her hand like she's waving me away. "At least I have people to invite to the party today. I mean, aside from the original nut job that is Uncle Max."

"And Eli," I tell her.

"Eli doesn't know any better, because he's the new kid. That's the only reason he's your friend at all."

"There are LOTS of reasons he's my friend," I say.

"Oh yeah?" Quinn counters. "Name one."

Okay, truthfully, I'm not exactly sure why Eli is my friend. But I'm not about to admit that!

"There's nothing special about you," Quinn adds.

"GET OUT!" I shout.

Quinn looks me square in the eye. "Make me," she says.

"You asked for it," I say, and I make a

pushing gesture with my hands, like I'm threatening to shove her or something. Man, I'd like to. She deserves it, after all: If you barge into the bathroom to spy on your brother, then you *should* be knocked over. But if I tried to hit Quinn, she'd just hit me back harder. She's strong that way.

And all of a sudden, she's swept off her feet.

I didn't touch her, I swear. She tripped over nothing, all on her own. Now she's on the floor, right on her butt.

"I see London, I see France, I see Quinn Cooley's underpants," I chant.

But Quinn doesn't seem to care. "Whoa," she says softly, her voice shaky. "Did you feel that?"

Before I can answer, Mom's in the doorway, her arms full of party decorations. "You're starting with each other already?" she says. "I thought we all agreed we were going to make this day a good day."

That had been part of the dinner conversation last night: "Let's not have any fights tomorrow," Mom had said. "Let's make it a good day." Though,

Quinn and I hadn't actually *agreed* to that.

"You all right, Quinn?" Mom asks. She puts the streamers on the counter and reaches a hand down to pull her up. Then she turns to me, accusingly. "Did you do this?"

"Uh-uh, no way," I say. "Quinn tripped all by herself. After she just marched right on in here– even though the door was closed."

"But not locked," Quinn says, straightening her skirt. "And whose fault is that?"

"She didn't even knock first," I say.

"I had to go. And Zack was taking forever."

"Oh, for Pete's sake, just use my bathroom," Mom tells her.

In the background, the phone rings.

"Work it out, you two," Mom tells us before grabbing the streamers and heading back down the hall to answer the phone.

"Thanks for getting me in trouble with Mom, nut job," Quinn says. But then she leaves, too. Finally.

I close the door behind her. Now I'm alone in the bathroom, but it's not like I actually need to be in here anymore.

Another day in the life of Zachary Cooley.

Leave it to Quinn to ruin everything.

2

UNCLE MAX

Two hours later the party is in full swing.

Quinn has twelve friends here. More than anyone needs, if you ask me. She's always jabbering away to them on the phone. Always. First there's her best friend, Bella, who doesn't even live in our town anymore. Her parents sent her away to some fancy boarding school. But she Skypes with Quinn every night–sometimes twice. Then Quinn has to Skype with everyone else she knows and report what Bella's up to, and how she's wearing her hair now, and whatever other completely pointless things girls talk about.

It goes on and on for HOURS. Which is why I never get a chance to be on the computer myself. Even though I have *much* more important things to do, like look up home-accident report statistics and type up lists of safety tips. All in the name of keeping my family safe.

But when I want to use the computer, Quinn just whines to Mom about it, and Mom takes her side and says I have to stop worrying so much about statistics and safety tips. She says I should concentrate on making friends, like Quinn does. As if having a few dozen friends is the most important thing. Friendship should be about quality, not quantity.

And I have quality ones—four of them—at the party today. Here, I'll list them in reverse order of importance:

Numbers four and three are my cousins, Will and George. Okay, I had to invite them, because their mom was my dad's younger sister. But still, they're here, so they count.

Number two is Eli, my best friend from school. (Fine, he's my only friend. Like I said, it's about quality, not quantity.)

By the way, it's not true what Quinn said, that Eli's my friend just because he's new and doesn't know better. He started at our school two months ago. That's not new anymore. It's certainly enough time to decide who you want to be friends with, and he's still friends with me.

Eli and I would have more friends in school if only the other boys in the fifth grade weren't such *Reggs*.

Reggs: Noun. Kids whose parents wish they could give them back, because they're such rotten eggs.

Quinn only invited girls to her party, so, thankfully, none of the Reggs are here. Though Quinn and her slame friends are starting to like the Reggs. I can tell by the way they giggle whenever the Reggs are up to their rotten tricks. Like when Newman, the worst of the Reggs, stuck a "Kick Me" sign on the back of Miss Kipnick, the cafeteria lunch lady. It's the oldest trick in the book, and it's not even a funny one.

Finally, my number one friend who I invited today: Uncle Max.

Uncle Max isn't really my uncle. We just call him that because he's known our family for so long. He knew Mom when she was a little girl, and he knew her father before that, and even his father before that. As usual, he's a little bit late today. He gets tied up with work stuff sometimes. He's so old, you'd think he would've retired by now. But he says he likes his job too much to give it up. He's a consulting transponder, which means he is in charge of communicating signals to receivers. To be honest, I don't really understand what he does. I just know it means he has to travel a lot. But he wouldn't miss my birthday. Birthdays are important to him. Mine even more than Quinn's, because I'm his favorite.

Not that Uncle Max has ever actually told

me I'm his favorite. In fact, he says Quinn and I are equally important to him. But isn't that just what an adult would say if he had a favorite and didn't want to go spreading it around? Uncle Max himself has told me you have to look beyond what people tell you. You even have to look beyond what they think is true, because sometimes they don't even know themselves.

So I looked beyond. And it's so obvious I'm right, it's almost embarrassing for him. First of all, there are our Tuesday and Thursday hangouts. Every week, without fail (unless Uncle Max has a business trip), he has standing plans with me. We go for long walks and talk about stuff, man-to-man. He's taken me to the amusement park a bunch of times, too. Uncle Max is always trying to get me on the Speed of Light roller coaster. But do you know roller coasters kill an average of four people each year? It's true. I looked it up. That's why I prefer the carnival games. You don't have to risk your life whooshing around in the air, and sometimes you even win prizes.

Quinn says she doesn't want to come to the amusement park with us. *Well, good, Quinn, because I don't remember anyone inviting you.*

Second of all, Uncle Max always gives me a better birthday present than he gives to Quinn. Last year he gave Quinn a series of books about a girl living in New York City. But he gave *me* a weekend trip to the city itself! We went to the biggest toy store I'd ever been to, and we went to the Empire State Building, which is a-hundred-and-two-stories tall. Uncle Max wanted to go up to the top, but I said no. It was too dangerous, for a lot of reasons. Not the least of which is the Empire State Building has a lightning rod at the top that gets struck by lightning twenty-three times a year. As far as I know, no *person* visiting the building has been struck by lightning. But it's not like you can predict where lightning will strike. That's why it's so dangerous, and it's better to stay on the ground and be safe instead of sorry.

I told Uncle Max it would be just as good to stand on the sidewalk and look up at the building stretching high into the sky above us. He argued for a bit, but in the end that's what we did.

When I'd looked at it for a good enough amount of time, I turned my head to tell Uncle Max I was ready to go back to the hotel and get dinner, but he was gone. I don't know exactly how it happened. One second he was right next to me; the next he wasn't. I had to get back to the hotel all on my own. Luckily, I'd memorized the address. You know, for safety reasons. I knew exactly where to go. I didn't talk to any strangers on the way. I just kept my head down and walked and walked and WALKED until my feet felt like they would fall off. When I finally got back, Uncle Max was in the lobby, waiting for me. He didn't look worried at all. "I knew you'd find your way," he told me, and he took me out for pizza.

I don't know what Uncle Max has planned for my present this year, but I've been angling for night-vision goggles. Sometimes at night, after everyone else has gone to bed, I like to walk through our house and do an inspection. I make sure no one has broken in while we've been sleeping, and I double-check that the front door, back door, and all the windows are locked. The problem is, it gets pretty dark in the hall, and I have to use a flashlight. Four times Mom has seen the light beams under her door, and four times she's gotten up and sent me straight back to bed, well before I finished my inspection. But if I had night-vision goggles, I wouldn't have to use the flashlight. I'd be able to keep everyone safe, and Mom wouldn't have to know.

I bet I get them, since I've dropped about a bajillion hints. And what will Uncle Max get Quinn? Hmmmm. Maybe regular swimming goggles. Maybe a case you can put your goggles in.

So even if most of the people in our backyard are here because of Quinn, and even if most of the presents in the pile by the back door are for her, I'm still excited.

In the meantime, Mom has us do all sorts of games, like an ice-cream-cone toss and a water-balloon relay. Both of which are harder than they sound, by the way. There's a points system to the day. First place for each event is ten points, second place is seven, and third place is five. In the end, whoever gets the most points wins the trophy.

"What's the score so far?" Quinn asks Mom.

"I haven't tallied the points up yet," Mom tells her.

"Did Uncle Max call to say when he's getting here?" I ask.

"I hope it's never," Quinn says.

"Oh, don't be that way," Mom says. "I know Uncle Max is a tad eccentric–"

"A *tad*?" she interrupts.

"But he's an important part of this family," Mom continues.

"He's not even *in* our family," Quinn argues.

"You just call him uncle because he was friends with Grandpa and the family has known him forever. But really he's just some random old guy."

"Are you guys talking about that man with the crazy hair and all the wrinkles who came to watch the talent show last month?" Quinn's friend Madeline asks. I'd had a harmonica solo in the talent show, which is why Uncle Max showed up. It's not like he cared about Quinn and her slame friends' choreographed dance. "He looks like Albert Einstein."

"Yeah, but not so smart," Quinn quips. "Just a nut job."

You see, another reason why I'm Uncle Max's favorite. Because Quinn is such a Regg herself when it comes to him.

"Shut up," I tell her.

"Zack, don't say that to your sister," Mom says. And before Quinn can gloat, Mom adds, "And cool it, Quinn. We don't call people names in this family."

"Sorry," Quinn says in a voice that is not at all sorry.

"That's better," Mom says. "I'm sure Uncle Max will be here any minute."

"We can do presents as soon as he's here, right?" I ask.

Mom starts to say yes, but then Quinn shouts, "Not if he gets here before the last game—the popcorn toss!"

"Mo-*om*!" I say.

I'd begged her to take the popcorn toss off the schedule. Here is how it goes: You pair off into teams of two. One person tosses the popcorn, and the other catches it in his or her mouth. Then they switch. Whoever catches the most wins.

But the problem is, if you catch a kernel at a wrong angle, it could get lodged in your throat and you'll choke!

"It's too dangerous," I say for about the hundredth time.

"It's not dangerous at all," Quinn tells Mom. "Zack just doesn't want to do it because he's no good at catching. Remember all those times Dad would throw a baseball and he'd drop it?"

I can hear Dad's voice in my head now: *Shake it off,* he'd said whenever I'd missed the ball. *Remember who you are–you're the one and only Zacktastic! Now let's try another one.*

I like being able to hear Dad's voice in my head, but sometimes it makes me miss him even more.

"If Zack can't catch with his hands, how does he expect to catch with his mouth?" Quinn goes on.

"That's not it," I insist to Mom. "I'm worried someone will choke to death."

Mom reaches forward to brush my hair off my forehead. She says she likes it better when she can see my eyes. "The kids will chew and swallow one kernel at a time," she tells me. "But you don't have to participate if you don't want to.

If you prefer, you can count what everyone else catches."

"No way!" Quinn says. "He'll cheat!"

"I'm not the cheater," I say.

If anyone is a cheater, it's Quinn. I bet she made Mom include this activity because she knew I wouldn't do it, so I'd lose.

"Your brother can count," Mom tells Quinn firmly.

And so it begins. I count—and listen for the slightest cough. Eli counts, too—I don't need his help counting, but he doesn't have anything else to do, since he doesn't have a popcorn partner without me.

So far Madeline is winning. She's caught ten kernels of popcorn in a row that Quinn has tossed her. Now eleven. Now twelve. It's going so fast, I don't think she's really chewing and swallowing them. In my head I picture all the kernels piling up in her throat—like a big popcorn ball that's going to get bigger and bigger until it explodes.

Next up is kernel number thirteen. I've always heard thirteen is an unlucky number. I'm not sure why, but suddenly it occurs to me: What if the thirteenth kernel is the most dangerous one?

Quinn pitches the thirteenth one toward Madeline. For a few seconds time seems to slow down, so I can see it all happening in slow motion. Madeline tips her head back. She opens her mouth wider. The kernel is sailing through the air and into Madeline's open mouth. I can practically see it go down her throat and get lodged in a bad place, blocking her windpipe along with all those other kernels she didn't chew and swallow properly.

My heart is pounding, but no one else seems concerned. Quinn is all set to throw the fourteenth kernel. "No!" I say.

"Zack, calm down," Mom says.

But Madeline is waving her hands in the air, signaling Quinn to stop. Her face is turning red. No, wait. It's not red. It's turning blue!

"Are you okay?" Mom asks.

"Madeline! Madeline!" Quinn runs to her side. So do the other kids.

"Give her space," I tell everyone in my sternest voice, and I guess because they're all scared, they do exactly what I say and back away.

Madeline's face is purple by now. She's choking, no doubt about it. Luckily, I'd watched a YouTube video about how to do the Heimlich maneuver, so I know what to do. I step behind her and wrap my arms around her middle, leaning against her and tipping her forward just slightly. The other kids and Mom are gathered like parentheses around us, but I pay no attention to them. I'm only concentrating on Madeline. I ball my right hand into a fist and position it just above where her belly button should be. Then I grab my fist with my left hand and press hard into her abdomen to try to force the popcorn out.

"Don't hurt her!" Quinn cries.

I push again and again and again. It takes five

times, but finally Madeline coughs. I let her go and feel my whole body exhale as the offending thirteenth piece of popcorn pops back out of her mouth.

Quinn rushes forward. "Are you okay?" she asks.

"Oh yes, she's okay now," Mom says. She sounds like she's trying to calm herself down as much as she's calming Madeline. She's stepped forward, too, rubbing Madeline's back as Madeline keeps on coughing. Out comes another piece of popcorn. Cough, and another. Cough, and another.

"Madeline?" Quinn says, her voice quavering.

"It's all right," Mom says. "As long as she's coughing, she's not choking anymore."

I know she's right about that because that's what it had said on the YouTube video: As long as someone is coughing, their airway isn't blocked.

"You did a good thing, Zack," Mom tells me.

I look over at Quinn, waiting for her to say

good job, too, and maybe even *thank you*. Bonus points if she admits I was right about the popcorn contest being a bad idea in the first place. But of course she doesn't. Meanwhile, Madeline coughs and coughs and coughs. Pretty soon there are dozens of kernels all over the lawn.

"It's the strangest thing," I tell Eli quietly. "I only counted thirteen when she was swallowing them."

"Me too," Eli says.

"Obviously there were more," Quinn says loudly. "At least a hundred. She broke a record!"

"I'm not sure about that," Mom admits.

"But look at the ground!"

Mom looks down, and I see her eyes widen at all the kernels peppering the grass like seashells at the beach. She shakes her head, but I can tell she thinks it's strange. "Zack, why don't you get Madeline some juice," she says.

I don't know why I should get the juice and not Quinn, since I'm the one who saved

Madeline's life, and Quinn is the one who did exactly nothing. But I go to the side table with the balloons strung up next to it, and I swipe a juice box to bring to Madeline. She downs it in nearly one gulp.

"Go easy," Mom tells her.

"She's lucky I was here, wasn't she, Mom?" I say. "Can you imagine if I was inside, or if I hadn't watched that Heimlich video?"

"I don't even *want* to imagine," Mom admits.

Madeline drains the last of the juice from the juice box. "I guess I should say thank you," she tells me. Her face is red when she says it. I'm pretty sure it's not from choking but because she's embarrassed about the whole thing.

"Or maybe not," Quinn says. "Maybe he distracted you with all his loud counting and it was all his fault!"

"I was counting in a perfectly normal voice," I say. "You're the one who insisted on the stupid popcorn contest in the first place—which means it's *your* fault. She could have *died!*"

"It's all right, Zack," Mom says. "All's well that ends well. Let's get back to the party business. We'll just disqualify this contest, which makes . . ." Mom pauses and looks down at her points tally. "Annie the grand prize winner of the day! Congratulations, Annie!"

Everyone echoes congratulations to Annie. Even Madeline, who has pretty much recovered, as far as I can tell. I'm watching her closely–her face is back to its regular color, and her breathing is totally normal. She's not coughing at all anymore, but I hear her mumble to herself, "I really wished I would win."

"Too bad for her, you don't get things just because you wish for them," Eli whispers to me.

I nod in agreement. If you ask me, Madeline should be grateful she's alive and not be so worried about winning. But I don't have any time to concern myself with her priorities, because suddenly there's an itch that starts on my right foot's big toe. I squirm all my toes around to make it stop, but it just gets worse. I drop down, pull off my sneaker, and scratch my toe through my sock. But it's not working. So then I pull off my sock and–

"Zack! Ew!" Quinn screams. "Mo-*om!*"

Mom looks down at me on the ground. "What on earth are you doing?"

"I think something bit me," I tell her. I hold my foot out to her so she can see my toe. "I hope it wasn't anything poisonous. Do you know how many people die each year because of poisonous insect bites?"

"You're *not* dying, Zack," Mom says.

I look back at my toe. I have to admit that it looks normal. Aside from the little birthmark that's always been there, a squiggle and a dot, there's nothing there. No bite.

So why is it itching so much? Is it possible there's an *invisible* bite on my toe? Invisible bites may be more dangerous. . . .

"Pee yew," Quinn says loudly. She holds her nostrils closed. When she talks, it sounds like she has a cold. "You're stinging ub da whole backyard wid dat ding."

"Huh?"

She unplugs her nose for just as long as it takes her to say, "You're stinking up the whole backyard with that thing!"

That *thing* is my *foot*. I kick my leg up so it's almost in her face. She drops her hand again to bat my foot away.

"Gross!" she cries.

"Zack, really," Mom says.

It can't be that bad. I lower my leg to smell it myself. I can't help but cringe because, well, my foot is a bit smellier than average.

I sniff again. There's something strangely likeable about the smell of your own smelly feet. The only word I can think of to describe it is *goodsgusting*.

Goodsgusting: Adjective. When something

smells good and disgusting at the same time.

"You don't even smell human," Quinn tells me.

"You don't even look human," I retort.

"All right," Mom says. "I think we've had enough drama for one day. Zack, go get the calamine lotion. It's in the hall closet."

Ah, yes. Calamine lotion. If there is something dangerous about an invisible bite, the lotion might neutralize the poison. I rub an extra amount on, like half the bottle. Then I put my sock back on and my shoe over it. It's kind of squishy as I walk back to the yard.

I spot Uncle Max standing by the fence and rush toward him to say hello. "How's the birthday so far?" he asks.

"It's a long story," I tell him.

But I don't have time to fill him in, because Mom says it's time for presents. Quinn and I always save the best for last. The difference is, I always save my Uncle Max present for the end, but Quinn opens hers first. She spots it right away, wrapped up in a brown burlap sack. Uncle Max doesn't believe in using wrapping paper. It's too wasteful, he says. Besides, it's what's inside that counts.

Quinn pulls out a silver jewelry box, her initials engraved on the top. It's definitely the best present he's ever given her. Not that she really cares, since it's from Uncle Max. "Thanks," she says after Mom prompts her.

We take turns, so next I open my present from Eli. Then Quinn takes a turn, then I open the present from Will and George. Quinn's turn again. I open my present from Mom and wait for Quinn.

And then.

My turn.

But there's nothing else with my name on it. Nothing wrapped in newspaper or tinfoil or even Saran wrap. Apparently Uncle Max didn't get anything for me.

I guess I'm not his favorite after all.

Unfortunately, I still have to sit through Quinn opening up ALL the rest of her presents. If I had to describe the experience, I'd say it's like watching the world's most boring movie–in slooooooooow motion. First Quinn holds up the package so she and her slame friends can *ooh* and *aah* over it. *Ooh, it's a box. Aah, it's covered in wrapping paper.* Like they've never seen a birthday present before. Like there aren't twenty others on the pile where that one came from. Then Quinn takes whatever ribbon or bow there is off the package and puts it aside to save. She slips her finger under the tape and lifts it up very gently, and then pulls the paper off. Her slame friends squeal like she did something difficult and important. Meanwhile, Quinn folds the paper up into a perfect square and puts it in a pile. And when all of that is said and done, finally, she looks at her present.

At this moment, Quinn is unwrapping her

five billionth present. Okay, maybe not actually the five billionth, but it's taking so long that it sure seems like it. Plus, it's a total fire hazard to have so many presents piled up around us. What if flames erupted and we needed to escape the backyard but everyone tripped over Quinn's loot and fell down and couldn't make it to safety?

I start to shove everything to the side. "Zack, stop, it's not yours!"

"I was just cleaning up," I say. "For safety reasons."

"All right, all right," Mom says. "Zack, stay on your side. Quinn, on yours."

Behind me, I hear someone go, *Humphhhh.*

When I turn around, there's Uncle Max shaking his head, his shaggy hair flopping from one side to the other. "Think of all the trees that were sacrificed just to wrap up the presents you and Quinn got today."

"Mostly Quinn," I mutter.

"If there's one thing I've learned in all my

years," he goes on, "it's that you can't go back and capture what once was. You can only go forward and live with the consequences."

I give my own *humphhhh*. I can't believe he's this upset about wrapping paper. It's like the wrapping paper is more important to him than I am. Mom will recycle it anyway, which Uncle Max knows. He's the one who brought over our three recycling bins–one for paper, one for plastic, and one for cans. He made us promise to always sort our garbage and never get lazy about it.

Quinn is finally done, and it's time for cake.

Twenty-one candles have been lit: ten each for Quinn and me, and one for us to grow on. Everyone sings the "Happy Birthday" song.

"Nut job," Quinn mutters under her breath.

"Slame," I mutter under mine.

"Make a wish!" Mom calls when the song ends. She's holding up her camera to get her annual picture of Quinn and me standing together, blowing out our candles. In all the photos around our house, it looks like Quinn and I actually like each other.

That's the thing about photos. They don't always tell you what it's like in real life.

My toe burns. And something else is burning inside of me, too. I'm upset that I didn't have a bunch of friends to invite to my party. And I'm upset that I didn't have a big pile of presents to prove it. And I'm upset that the one person I count on the most didn't even bother to bring me anything.

Where is Uncle Max now? I scan the backyard, but he's nowhere to be seen. Well, that figures. Quinn's friends are chanting, "Quinn! Quinn! Quinn!" Like she's the only one having a birthday.

I bend my head toward the cake to get the candle-blowing part over with. I know most of the group will be clapping for Quinn—not me. It's like I'm not having a birthday at all. For a second I imagine the candles exploding. That'd stop their chanting for sure.

"Zack!" Mom suddenly screams.

I look up again. "What?"

"Your face—it looked like it was on fire."

I touch my fingers to my cheeks, and the skin feels smooth and normal. But maybe this tradition is too dangerous. Kids all over the world are leaning too close to fire on their birthdays. I take a step back. "Come on," Quinn says impatiently.

"Don't lean too close," I tell her.

"Don't tell me what to do."

"All right," Mom says. "Let's try this again. Make a wish, kids—and be careful."

And so I do make my wish. Then I lean forward—not too far forward—and blow.

3

THE GIFT

After the party, Quinn and I each get to have a friend stay for a little while. Quinn invited Madeline. I invited Eli, but he has to go visit his dad. His parents are divorced. That's why he moved to our town, Pinemont, in the first place. His dad lives an hour away, in Philadelphia, which is a big city. Eli sees him every other weekend. This is technically his dad's weekend, but he was allowed to stay at his mom's long enough to go to my party. My cousins also had to leave, because it's a long drive back to their house on Long Island.

I thought at least I'd have Uncle Max to hang out with. But after the whole present thing, I'm not so sure I want to.

Uncle Max is in the den with Mom, and I head into my room with my presents. There's the keyboard from Will and George, which is cool because now I can add a musical element to my safety reports. But I don't feel like doing that now. Eli got me a microscope. I stick my finger under the lens and examine it. Blown up, the lines of my fingerprint look like worms, or a maze. And then there's my last present, from Mom. It's a watch, just like the one Dad used to wear. I put it on. It makes my wrist look more mature. Like my dad's, except his wrist was hairier.

There's a knock at my door. "Can I come in?" calls a voice. Uncle Max's voice.

"I guess," I say.

"Can I sit down?" he asks when he steps into the room.

"Sure."

He sits. "Anything you want to talk about?"

Yes, I want to say. *When did Quinn start being your favorite?* "No," I say instead.

And then I notice that he's holding something. Some kind of box. Or not a box, exactly. A towel, kind of bulky like there's something inside it. It's folded up and secured with safety pins.

That's just the way Uncle Max would wrap a present for someone, if he had one to give.

"Is that for me?" I ask.

Uncle Max nods and hands it over. "I wanted to give it to you in private."

"I knew you wouldn't really forget me," I say. Even though I hadn't known that, and if you want to know the truth, I wish I'd found that out in front of the other kids. I would've liked them to at least see me get a really cool present, no matter how private it is.

But this is no time to worry about all of that. I unhook the pins (and recap them so they won't prick anyone), and unwind the towel. "Careful," Uncle Max says.

"I know," I say. You have to be careful with night-vision goggles. The lenses are made of glass, and if you break them, they won't work. Plus, the shards of glass could be sharp and cut you. If a cut is bad enough, you could die. Or at least need stitches.

The towel is unwound. My present is in my lap. It's not goggles. It's not even a silver box like Quinn got. It's a bottle.

A scratched-up old green bottle that you definitely wouldn't pick up if you found it washed up on the beach. The letters SFG are engraved on the side. They must be someone's initials, but they're not mine. Which means the bottle used to belong to someone else. Which means it's a used gift. Even Quinn got something new from Uncle Max. You could tell because they were her initials engraved into the silver jewelry box.

There's no top on my "new" used bottle. Whatever was once in it is gone, and it's empty now. I turn it over in my hands. The number SEVEN and the word PORTAL are engraved on the bottom.

"You know what it is?" Uncle Max asks.

"A bottle," I tell him. Duh.

What am I supposed to do with a bottle? A *used* one at that. I guess it's a good thing I didn't open this in front of Quinn and her friends after all. But just because Uncle Max spared me the humiliation of the World's Worst Present in front of the other kids doesn't make me feel any better.

He nods. "It's for genies."

"Geniuses?"

Even if I am a genius, I still wish Uncle Max had gotten me a better present.

Sorry, that might be rude. But it's the truth.

"Genies," Uncle Max repeats, this time a beat slower and a decibel louder. "You know what they are, right?"

"Of course," I say. I've seen the movie *Aladdin*. The kid rubbed the bottle, out came a big blue genie, he got three wishes, and . . .

Wait a second.

"Are you saying you got me a genie? Because I'm ten now. I don't believe in make-believe things anymore. In fact, I stopped believing in them a long time ago."

"You need to open your mind a bit more."

"Open my mind to believing there's a genie in this bottle? I'm not that gullible."

"No, there's no genie in the bottle. Not now anyway."

"What do you mean?"

"Zack," Uncle Max says, looking more serious than I've ever seen him look. "You *are* the genie."

4

It Ain't Just a River in Egypt

A genie?

A bottle-dwelling, wish-granting, all-around magical genie?

Yeah, right.

I break into a grin. "Oh, Uncle Max, come on."

"This isn't a joke," he says, with that serious look still on his face.

But I'm onto his plan: He's going to try to get me to believe this unbelievable story, and then he'll burst out laughing and hand me my *real* present. The goggles, I'll bet.

I lean over and try to peer around Uncle

Max. I don't *see* any other package. He must have it hidden in another room.

Maybe it's something even better than night-vision goggles. My mind races with things that could possibly be better. Walkie-talkies, so I can communicate with my family when we're not in the same room. Or fire extinguishers for every room. Or . . . Or . . .

Or a dog! A guard dog to help me look after the house. I'll name him Buddy, or maybe Crackerjack. He'll love me more than anyone else—especially more than Quinn, and he'll sit close to me on the couch when I'm doing my homework or watching TV. At night he'll sleep in my bed, except for the times he leaves to patrol the halls and check for strangers. If he sees any, he'll grab on to their legs and not let go until the police arrive.

Uncle Max could be hiding my new dog somewhere in our house, or maybe it's back at his place. Either way, he's not letting on that there's any other present hiding anywhere.

Fine, I'll play along. "So," I say to Uncle Max, "people rub this bottle and I pop out, just like that?"

"Something like that," he says.

"But I'm already *outside* the bottle right now," I point out.

Poor Uncle Max. He didn't really think this joke all the way through.

"When the time comes, you'll be pulled into the bottle," he says.

I don't bother pointing out that I'm about four hundred times the size of the bottle.

"And then what? I'll pop out and grant three wishes to whoever rubbed the bottle, like in *Aladdin*?"

"You know about Aladdin?"

"Of course I do. Everyone's seen that movie."

"Oh. That movie," Uncle Max says, spitting the words out like they taste sour. He shakes his head, and a clump of his thick white hair falls in front of his face, obscuring his left eyeball. "It got a few things wrong–more than a few things. You know Hollywood–they take a nugget of the truth and twist it around to make it ridiculous."

I don't know a thing about Hollywood. But come on. "You're saying you think there were nuggets of actual truth in the movie–that it got some things right?"

Uncle Max nods gravely. "There *are* genies," he says. "They travel through bottles that serve as portals. Do you know what a portal is?"

"Sure," I say.

"Okay. What is it?"

"Umm," I say. I didn't expect Uncle Max to quiz me. "I forget."

"Well, I'll tell you, and I think you should commit this to memory. A portal is an entry port."

"Okay."

"Think of it as a doorway," he continues. "You go in one portal and come out another. It's the genie mode of transportation."

"That'd be cool if it were true," I tell him.

"Trust me, Zack, the truth about genies is cooler and more exciting than anything you've seen in some silly little cartoon. And now you're a part of it."

I shake my head. I can't help it.

"There are several stages to finding out you're a genie," Uncle Max says. "The first one is denial. It's true what they say–it ain't just a river in Egypt."

"Huh?"

"Just an expression. The Nile. Denial. Anyway, what I mean is you're right on schedule. Your reaction is typical."

Never in all of my ten years has Uncle Max ever called me typical.

"Come on," I say. "Give it up already. This whole thing you're describing is impossible–being a genie, and granting wishes, and getting sucked up into one bottle and popping out of another."

"Very few things are impossible," Uncle

Max says. "Very few things indeed. That's lesson number one."

"Plenty of things are impossible," I say, starting to tick things off my fingers. "For example, a car transforming into a horse, then into a zebra–"

"Lesson number two," he says, ignoring me. "I've never lied to you."

"Then into a dinosaur," I continue. "A real, live one that you can ride."

Not that I'd ride a dinosaur. Or even a horse. Do you know how many people break their backs and die each year from falling off animals?

"All right, Zack," Uncle Max says. "I get the picture. Car, horse, zebra, dinosaur. Let's you and I get out of here."

He calls to Mom and Quinn that we're heading over to his house. Mom says, "Have a good time." Quinn doesn't say anything. I bet she and Madeline are taking inventory of all the stuff Quinn got today.

Uncle Max's house is four blocks away. When we get there, we sit down on the porch swing in the back. He carried the bottle with him, tucked under his arm like a football.

A football would've been a better birthday gift. And I don't even play sports. Not since before Dad, well . . . The point is, I don't play anymore, because there are too many injuries. And I'd *still* rather have a football than an old, scratched-up used bottle.

"This bottle," Uncle Max begins. "Now that I've given it to you, you have to take care of it."

"No offense," I say, "but it doesn't look like the previous owner took such good care of it." SFG, whoever he was, nicked it up real good. "And that's another thing you're getting wrong, by the way," I tell him. "They used a lamp in the movie."

"And I suppose that movie is the source of all your information on genies," Uncle Max says. "Well, just so you know, stories about genies go back further in time than anything you see in the movies or on television. They go back further than movies or TV shows themselves."

I wave him off. "Yeah, sure."

"Zack, look at me," Uncle Max says. I look at him–at his wild white hair, his curly mouth, his bright candy-colored shirt. "Have I ever lied to you?"

It's true. He may have wacky hair and talk kind of fast and show up late sometimes. But he's no liar. He told me the truth about getting your blood drawn: It hurts, no matter how tiny the needle is. He told me the truth about liver: It may be good for you, but it tastes disgusting.

And he told me the truth about my dad. All the other adults around me were acting like he'd recover and life would go back to normal. But it was Uncle Max who'd told me Dad was hurt bad, so bad that he wasn't going to get better. He was going to die, and life would never be the same again.

So maybe he's not lying now, either.

Suddenly I get it. And what I get makes me really sad.

"Well?" Uncle Max says, waiting.

"You always tell me to look beyond what people say," I tell him. He nods. "So the thing is, uh . . ."

"Yes?"

How can I explain this?

"You're kind of, well, old," I tell him.

Not even kind of. Uncle Max is really and truly old. He won't tell anyone his real age. If someone asks him, he just says, "I'm as old as the rest of me." Whatever that means.

I don't think about Uncle Max's age so much because he acts young. Most old men are retired, not transponding, or whatever it is he does at his job. And they're not riding roller coasters, either, or running around New York City all day without getting tired. But right now I'm noticing just how deep the lines on Uncle Max's forehead are, as if they'd been carved that way. And he has so many crinkles at the corners of his eyes, I can't even count them all.

"No offense," I continue. "It's not that I think you're lying about this genie business. But maybe you're confused. I heard that can happen to old people."

Uncle Max makes the *humphhhh* sound again. I guess I hurt his feelings. I feel bad about that. But more than that, I feel worried. People die from old age. There's nothing anyone can do about it.

"Take off your shoe," Uncle Max says.

"Huh?"

"Your right shoe. Take it off."

"All right," I say. I take it off.

"The sock, too," he says.

"Okay."

My sock used to be white, but it's turned pink from soaking up the calamine lotion. I peel it off, and Uncle Max reaches for my foot. He

57

pinches the big toe between his fingers. At least he doesn't care about how badly my foot stinks. Or that it's pink and slippery. "You see this mark," he says, "right here?"

I've had that squiggle, sort of like a backward S with a dot on top, my whole life. "My birthmark? Sure, I see it."

"That's a genie bite."

"Now you're saying a genie bit me?"

"No, that's just what that mark is called," he says. "You're right that it's been there since birth–I checked both you and Quinn when you were born. The shape it takes indicates your genie age." He pokes some more at my toe. "This shape means ten. So sometime during the year you're ten, your powers will emerge."

My voice is supersoft, almost a whisper, when I say, "Uncle Max, I think you need to see a doctor. I think you have that Old Timer's disease."

"You mean Alzheimer's?"

Is that what it's called? "Yeah, you should

really talk to someone about it."

"Is that so?" he asks.

I nod miserably. Mr. Walden, my science teacher at Pinemont Elementary, is fond of saying the most likely answer is usually the correct one. And what's more likely in this case? That I'm a genie or that Uncle Max is sick and mistaken?

"Well, okay then," Uncle Max says. "I figured it would come to this."

"Come to what?" I ask.

But instead of answering, he licks a finger and twirls it in the air. "Watch your foot," he tells me.

Why is Uncle Max so obsessed with my foot? Is that something that happens right before an old person dies? I'm so worried about him, and I don't know what to do.

If Dad were here, *he'd* know what to do.

Mom is the next best thing. I should go inside and call her. Better yet, I should run home. I'm about to put my shoe back on and race to her when I notice something: The mark on my big toe has turned bright purple. It's been pale pink my whole life. Could it be a reaction to the calamine lotion? I've never heard of an allergic reaction that turns birthmarks different colors.

Wait, now it's blue. I blink a bunch of times really fast, and now it looks like it's flecked with glitter. I press the balls of my hands hard onto my eyeballs. When I remove them, my whole foot is shining like there's a lightbulb inside of it.

My heart is *boom-boom-boom*ing in my chest. I want to scream, but my voice is caught in my throat. What's happening to me? Is my foot going to fall off next? Or worse–am I gonna die? People can die from allergic reactions, you know.

I turn toward Uncle Max. He's changed. His white hair is combed smooth and slicked back; his mouth is set straight. Everything about him seems polished and powerful. It's him, but it's not him.

"Check it out, over there," Uncle Max says.

Holy smokes! There's a car on the lawn! When did that get here? Now it's turning into a

horse, and I'm hurling through the air toward it. I manage to land squarely on its back. It starts running around in a circle, faster and faster, and I'm clutching on for dear life. Beneath me, the horse changes to a zebra, then to a dinosaur.

A dinosaur? That's impossible! This is all impossible!

"Car, horse, zebra, dinosaur—wasn't that it?" Uncle Max says, cackling.

I'm hanging on to the dino's neck as tightly as I can. It slows to a trot, then stops completely. Then *poof,* it's gone, and I fall to the ground. Uncle Max is at my side. He scratches his hair with his fingers, and it's back to its floppy style.

"So you're a . . . ," I say. "You're a . . ." I can't even get the word out.

"Genie," he finishes for me. "Yes, I am."

5

Anger and Bargaining

"Since when?" I ask.

"Since I was born," he says. "But my powers emerged when I was fourteen, just as yours are starting to now."

"So that means you've been lying to me for my whole life?"

"I've never told you anything that wasn't true."

"You didn't tell me anything at all."

"I'm telling you now."

Like that makes up for everything. I don't know what to think or feel. My head feels heavy with too much information. "You could've killed me!" I practically shout.

Uncle Max shakes his head. "Nonsense. I've only come close to killing someone once, and that's a story for another time," he says. "Now, about the gift I just gave you—"

"Oh, no," I say, cutting him off. "I am NOT living inside that thing."

"Zack," Uncle Max starts.

"No way," I tell him. "No how. I'd never get to see my friends!"

In the back of my head I can hear Quinn's voice saying, *But, Zack, you don't have any friends.*

"And how would I eat?" I go on. "And what about . . . what about when I have to go to the bathroom?"

If my feet smelled bad, the inside of that bottle would be ripe!

"It's not like a genie could fit a toilet in there," I say.

"Slow down and look at me," Uncle Max says. "*I'm* not living in a bottle, am I?"

"No, but–"

"Listen, what you're feeling right now is perfectly normal. You're in the anger stage, the second stage of finding out you're a genie."

"I have every right to be angry! I just found out you've been keeping the world's biggest secret from me–that I'm going to have to spend the rest of my life granting other people's wishes. Unless that part of the movie isn't the way it happens in real life."

"No, that part is true. But here's something that's also true: You're now a part of something much bigger than just yourself. If you could only see that."

"What if I don't want to be part of anything bigger? What if I just want to be myself–the exact version of myself that I was yesterday, and the day before that, and the day before that? Shouldn't I get a say in this? I mean, why is this even happening to me? I'm not that . . . I'm really not that . . ."

My voice trails off, but here's what I'm thinking: *Quinn is right. I'm really not that special.*

"Can't you take it back?" I ask softly. "Make me not a genie, please."

"I can't take it back from you any more than I can take it back from myself," Uncle Max says. He slips his right foot out of his sandal and shows me a wavy circle on his own big toe. I'd never noticed it before. "This is my genie bite."

"Wait a second–I caught being a genie from you? Like it's some kind of disease?"

"No, no, it's not catching," Uncle Max says. "It's passed down through family bloodlines."

"I can't get anything from your bloodline if we're not related," I remind him.

"Ah, but we are," he says. "I'm your great-grandfather, seven times over. Your mom doesn't know it. Her dad didn't know it, and his dad didn't know it. The genie gene usually skips a few generations. There was no reason to tell them the truth."

"So you *did* tell me something that wasn't true."

"I never actually told you that," Uncle Max says. "I just didn't contradict anyone when they told you I was an old family friend. I've been around too long for anyone to really keep track."

"Well, I'm keeping track, and that counts for lie number two! How many more are there?"

"Listen, Zack, it was the best way for me to stay in the family, stay in everyone's lives, without anyone suspecting anything. Not that they would suspect *this*. But I'm glad it's out in the open between us now. It's about time."

"Time? Time for you to die and leave this genie thing all to me?"

"I'm not dying. That's not how this works."

"So being a genie means I'll live forever? That's even worse! Everyone I know will die, and I'll still be here."

"Zack," Uncle Max says.

"No, this can't be true," I say. "It's just a dream.

A really, really bad dream. That's the only way this makes sense." I pinch myself to try to wake up, but that doesn't work. So then I look away from Uncle Max, up to the sky, like I'm praying. I should clasp my hands together. Okay, done. "If it's a dream, then I will be nice to Quinn," I say.

"Ah, the bargaining stage," Uncle Max says.

"I don't want to hear any more about stages!"

"Then hear this: Being a genie, granting wishes for other people, is a powerful job," Uncle Max explains. "There is value in power, as long as it's used wisely."

"But I–"

Hold up. Power has *value*? Does he mean like *money*? Will I be allowed to wish for things for myself? If that's the case, if genies can grant their own wishes, then shouldn't Uncle Max be rich? But his house is on the small side, and most of the stuff he has is pretty old.

Maybe he just hasn't wished for money. Maybe there isn't anything he really wants to buy. But I don't think there'd be anything wrong with wishing up a few things for myself. It's not like it'd hurt anyone else.

"Fine, I'll be a genie, but there has to be something in it for me. I have some wishes of my own, you know."

I'm starting to see the possibilities. I could conjure us up a great big house—one where Quinn and I each got our own bathrooms. Maybe we could each have our own staircases leading to our own rooms. Our own *suites*, I mean! Super big to fit everything I could ever want in the world, and I'd never even have to pass Quinn in the hall.

Forget night-vision goggles. I could buy a super high-tech surveillance system for the whole house with cameras everywhere connected to a wall of TV screens in my bedroom.

Or I could wish for a force field to be set up around our property so no one who's not invited could get in.

Or . . .

Holy smokes. I could wish for Dad. Go back in time and tell him, "Sure, I'll go run errands with you." He'd wanted me to go, and I'd said no because *Space Invasion* was on TV. That dumb show about fake people. I'll never watch it ever again. If I'd gone with Dad, if I'd changed that one little thing about that day, everything would have been different. We would've stopped for ice cream. He wouldn't have been at the wrong place at the wrong time, and the accident would never have happened.

Or maybe I don't need to go back in time. I'll just wish him back to life right now, and I can catch him up on the last two years myself.

I don't care which way it happens, just as long as I get him back.

"Do I make wishes out loud, and suddenly they'll be granted?" I ask. "Are there special wishing words?"

"You aren't the one who makes the wishes, Zack," Uncle Max tells me. "That isn't how it works."

"But, Uncle Max, that's not fair!"

"Fair doesn't have anything to do with it," he says. "But don't worry about that right now. What you need to understand at this moment is that you're in the seventh genie family. There are twelve genie families in this world, and we twelve are the only ones entrusted with this power—with this responsibility. It's our destiny."

"My destiny," I say. I've never thought about having a destiny before. I just thought you live your life the best you can and cross your fingers that bad things like car accidents don't happen to you.

"Yes, destiny," Uncle Max repeats. "Ten years old is a bit young to start your genie work—four whole years younger than I was—and this is a job that demands some maturity. You're going to learn a lot about people by what they wish for, sometimes more than they even know about themselves. I know you're a good kid, Zack, a smart kid, and this all needs to be handled with the utmost care. But we'll talk about all of this,

I promise. Meantime, in the next few weeks, strange things may start to happen. As your powers begin to emerge, you may feel a bit like a spark plug. You're a current of energy, and you don't know how to control it yet. You have to be careful, and–"

"When can I start making the magic happen?"

"All in due time, Zack. All in due time. But here's something I need to tell you now, and I can't say it strongly enough: You need to hang on to that bottle. You don't want it to end up in the wrong hands. That would be bad–very bad indeed."

"Uh-huh," I say.

"Unfortunately, there are evil forces in the world," he goes on. "I've done my best to keep this world safe from them. But you can never be too careful." Uncle Max pauses. "Zack, are you listening to me?"

"Yup. Bottle, evil forces, be careful."

"A little bit of distance can go a long way. Remember that."

"I'll remember," I say. "But wait—how am I supposed to keep my eyes on the bottle if I'm sucked up into it and spit out a different one? If they're portals, like you said."

"We call it sides of the bottle," Uncle Max explains. "You look out for this bottle when you're here, on this side. When you're called away to the other side on genie business, there'll be another bottle for you to keep a close eye on. It'll be your ticket home, too."

"Quinn's not going to believe this," I say.

"You can't tell Quinn about this," Uncle Max says.

"Oh, come on, *please*," I say. "Just a little bit. Or maybe I could do some sort of trick in front of her. You know, to prove it."

Quinn thinks she's so much cooler than I am. This will certainly show her!

"No, I mean you *can't* tell her," Uncle Max

says. "You're physically unable to. If you try telling anyone outside the genie world, the words that come out of your mouth won't make any sense. You'll just sound a bit strange until you change topics."

"How can I even be sure you're telling me the truth about that? Maybe you don't want me to tell Quinn, so you're telling me lie number three."

"You don't believe me?" Uncle Max asks. "Stay here. I'll be right back." He leaves me on the back porch and goes inside. A minute later he's back with a phone in his hand. "Here. Your sister is on the line for you."

I press it to my ear. "Uh, hi, Quinn."

"This better be important, Zack. Madeline and I are in the middle of doing spa treatments."

"It is," I promise. I pause to take a really deep breath in, and then I exhale out.

"Gross, I heard that!" Quinn shouts.

"What's gross about breathing?" I ask,

but then I change my mind. "Never mind. I have something to tell you. Something crazy. Something amazing. Something *crazmazing*!"

Crazmazing. Adjective. When something is crazy and amazing at the same time.

"Ugh," Quinn says. "Just spit it out. And use actual words that exist in actual dictionaries, please."

"Okay. I know you're not going to believe this. But I'm a genie."

"I'm not going to believe what?"

"I'm a genie," I repeat.

For a couple of seconds there's just silence. And then Quinn starts yelling: "Zachary Noah Cooley, I told you to use real words! But if you're just going to speak some fake alien language to me, then I'm hanging up the phone!" And that's what she does, without waiting for me to answer. The next thing I hear is a click and a dial tone. I lower the phone from my ear and look over at Uncle Max.

"I told you so," he says.

"Aw, man," I said. "That stinks!"

"Sorry, Zack," Uncle Max says. "It's a safety mechanism put in place by the Genie Board in the seventh parallel. Decision number two hundred and fifty-eight. We've had trouble in the past."

There's something called a *Genie Board*?

"Okay," I say. "Can I use some of my spark plug energy to do magic in front of her? Not accidental magic, though. Real stuff, just like you did to me. Then she'll totally believe me. Or maybe she won't, and she'll think she's turning into a nut job herself!"

"That's not the way you're supposed to use your power, Zack."

Not supposed to doesn't mean *not possible*.

"But you can come to me with any genie business," he continues. "*I'll* be able to understand you. And you *must* tell me if you feel anything out of the ordinary. Like if you have any strange sensations. Those tend to pop up when people make wishes around you. It's a little like an allergy. It'll be different than when you're actually called upon to grant wishes. But still, you should tell me about them when they occur."

"I had a strange itch today," I tell him. "Quinn's friend Madeline said she wished something. And by the way, my toe didn't itch a little bit. It itched like crazy."

"How crazy?"

"Like a hundred fire ants bit me in the same spot," I tell him.

"Hmm," Uncle Max says. "It's happening sooner than I thought. On Monday I'll make a call to SFG."

SFG? As in the initials on the bottle? Who could he–or she–be?

I don't have a chance to ask. "Uh, Uncle Max," I say. "Something's happening right now."

"Your toe is itching again?"

"No, it's not itchy. It feels . . . I don't know . . . it feels alive." I guess toes are always alive, as long as they're part of a living body. But when was the last time you were aware of the life in your toe? "It feels like it's about to take off."

Tingles travel from my toe up my whole body. Suddenly I'm lifted up. For *real*. I'm floating in the air, and spinning around and around and around. You know that pins-and-needles feeling you get when your foot falls asleep? That's what my whole body feels like. "What's happening to me?!"

"You're being called away for your first genie assignment," Uncle Max says. He's on the porch still. Standing up now, but *his* feet are still planted firmly on the ground.

"Aren't you coming with me?" I ask.

"A genie works alone," he says. "But I didn't think this would happen so soon."

"Uncle Max!"

"It's all right, Zack. It'll be all right. Just . . ."

His voice is fading away. I'm headed right toward the green bottle. It looks bigger than before. In fact, it looks gigantic. Did it grow? I whip my head toward Uncle Max, and he looks like a giant. Holy smokes, I'm shrinking! How small will I get? Down to nothing? I want to cry out, *Help me!* But my voice is gone.

"If you need me, call me through–" Uncle Max says.

But whatever the end of his sentence is, I don't hear it. I'm sucked inside the bottle instead.

6

Dumped

I'm twisting and turning and hurling superfast. This must be what the Speed of Light roller coaster feels like. My heart drops down to my stomach. My stomach is in my throat. And my throat, well, I don't know where it is. I can't feel it anymore. I can't even tell if I'm screaming, because the sound of wind is too loud in my ears. There are so many twists and kinks and turns— it's as if I'm traveling through someone's lower intestine.

They say the speed of light is the fastest speed there is. But this has got to be faster—even if that's not technically possible.

Very few things are impossible, Uncle Max had said.

Ah, I'm slowing down now. I feel myself being pushed out of something.

But *pushed* is the wrong word. It's more like I'm being *squeezed*. I have to suck in my stomach and hold my breath.

And I'm out.

There's no time to be relieved about it because I'm flying through I-don't-know-where. The sky? Outer space? I don't have time to look around before my body remembers there's such a thing as gravity, and *NOSEDIVE*!

I'm heading toward something dark and blue. It looks just like a lake. That is, if you're looking at a lake from high above.

Holy smokes! I'm heading toward a lake?!

It's getting closer. I don't know how to swim, which means I'm about to drown! I'm too young to die!

I squeeze my eyes shut, tight as I can. I can't bear to watch.

And then . . .

Nothing.

No smash, no splash. This doesn't mean I'm dead, does it? I don't *feel* dead–not that I know what being dead feels like. But I feel, well, *alive* still. And not like I'm nose-diving anymore. I open one eye, just a slit.

The dark blueness is right below me. I'm hovering above it. I guess gravity doesn't apply to genies after all. Man, that was close. Probably broke the record of closeness in the history of close calls.

I open my other eye. Hmmm. That's not water. It's . . . well, I don't know what it is. It's kind of, uh, cushiony looking. I reach out a teeny, tiny arm. But I'm not close enough to actually touch it.

The pins-and-needles feeling all over my body is back, and suddenly: *Pop!*

Whoa. That's my right hand. My GIANT right hand. Or maybe it's just back to the regular size, but it looks giant compared to the rest of me.

I can reach the blue now. It *does* feel like a cushion.

Pop! goes my left hand.

Pop! Pop! Pop! Just like popcorn kernels, my body's growing bigger in bits and pieces. One of my eyes bugs out before the rest of my face goes bigger, kind of like a bubble bursting out of my eye socket. I can't even imagine how strange I must look.

There's one last enormous pop, and I'm back to my same, wonderful, state-of-the-art Zack-body. And then *SPLAT!* The cushion breaks my landing, before I roll off it and onto the floor.

Oh, beloved floor! Glorious floor! Floor of solid ground! I could kiss you!

But that would be weird, so I don't.

Instead I do a quick inventory of my body. Fingers and toes: check! Eyes, nose, and mouth:

check! Two arms, two legs: check! I think I've got it all. Phew.

Now to figure out where I am exactly. I sit up and look around. On the far wall, colors are spiraling like pinwheels. I stand slowly, blinking, blinking, blinking. I realize I'm actually staring right into an enormous stained glass window as the afternoon sun glares through it. I spin around and see rows and rows of dark pews. That must be what I landed on: one of the dark-blue cushioned pews.

The last time I was in a place with cushioned pews was the chapel for Dad's funeral. My breath quickens once again. The *boom-boom*ing of my heart is back to full force.

There's a staccato *pop! pop!*–one pop on one side of my head, another on the other side. Oh, my ears are back. I hadn't realized they'd still been itty-bitty.

The first thing I hear is a scream: "OWWWWWWW! GET OFFA ME, YOU

DIRTBALLS!" Quickly, I duck back down to the ground, out of sight.

"Ooh, he's a slippery little sucker," a different voice says, presumably a dirtball. "Come back here, ya twerp!"

"Help me!"

Could this "twerp" be my genie assignment?

"Shut up!" shouts the dirtball.

"Yeah, twerp, you're the one who got us into this mess," yet another voice says. I'm betting it's dirtball number two.

Wait, who am I supposed to help? The twerp or the dirtballs?

I slide on my stomach, commando-style, in between the pews to the back of the chapel, where the voices are coming from.

Along the way I pass an overturned backpack and a trail of items strewn across the floor. Items that must've once been inside it: a broken pencil, a pen without the cap, notebooks flipped open and pages scrunched up, a couple of books, plus

an iPod, an iPad, and an iPhone. Holy smokes, that's a lot of electronics for one backpack. I don't have any of those things.

I see a hand reach out toward a blue binder.

"Oh, Trey-*ey*," one of the dirtballs calls, turning a one-syllable name into two. "Come out, come out, wherever you are."

"There he is!"

"Aha! Where do you think you're going, twerp?"

That's when I see him—Trey, aka the twerp. He's a skinny red-haired kid with glasses that are lying crooked across the bridge of his nose. One of the lenses is smashed up. Two larger boys pounce on top of him. By process of elimination, they must be the dirtballs. One has shaggy blond hair and freckles, and the other has a brown buzz cut. All three boys are wearing khaki pants and white button-down shirts, with MA stitched into their front pockets.

MA? Like for Massachusetts? But I live in Pennsylvania. I know from the map in Mrs. Hould's classroom that they're separated by at least a few states. It would take hours in the car to get there. Genie travel sure is quick.

"OWWWWWWW!" comes another scream. The shaggy blond kid has a tuft of red hair in his fist, and he's yanking hard. "Hey, you!" Trey calls. He's looking right at me. "Do something!"

Do something? What could I possibly do? Take on Shaggy and Buzz Cut? I may be a genie, but I don't know how to use my powers yet, and these guys are two of the worst Reggs I've ever seen. Plus, they're big–WAY bigger than I am.

"Who are you talking to?" Buzz asks.

"That kid over there," Trey says. "He's been watching you the whole time. You better let me go, or you guys are gonna get in so much trouble! Even more trouble than before!"

Buzz steps off Trey and looks in my direction. I barely have time to duck back behind the pews. "I don't see anyone," he reports.

"That's because the twerp is a lying liar," Shaggy says. "There's no one in here."

He tugs harder on Trey's hair. "OWWWW!" Trey cries. "You're hurting me!"

"Now, the question remains," Buzz says. "What should we do with this sniveling little twerp?"

"Let me go, let me go, let me GOOOOOO! Please, if you do it now, I won't tell anyone about this."

"You bet you won't," Shaggy says. "Or we'll

make life even worse for you."

"We could shut him inside a locker," Buzz suggests.

"Nah, that's so overdone," Shaggy replies. "Besides, once class is over, everyone'd come into the hall and hear him shouting to get out. How about if we stick him in the utility closet?"

"We don't have the keys to unlock it," Buzz says.

"Good point," Shaggy says.

Trey's pleas have lowered to a whimper: "Please, please, please."

"I've got it," Buzz Cut says with a snap. "We'll take him to the garbage dump. It has his name on it, after all."

"Jake, you're a frigging genius," Shaggy tells him.

There's a flurry of action as the Reggs climb off Trey. Shaggy starts to pick him up. Something rolls across the floor. It's a bottle. A green one. Scratched up just like mine.

"That's my bottle."

Uh-oh. Did I say that out loud? Luckily, my voice came out as barely a whisper. But Trey meets my eye again. Shoot, he heard me.

"No way," he says, loud enough for Shaggy and Buzz to hear, too. "*You're* my genie?!"

"Ha!" Shaggy spits out. "Did you just say *genie*?"

"Your daddy get one of those for you, too, twerp?" Buzz asks, barely suppressing his laughter.

"He did," Trey says, "and I wish–"

My toe starts itching again. That must mean Trey is the genie assignment. At least, I think that's what it means. I *hope* that's what it means. I'd much rather grant the wishes of a twerp than of a couple of Reggs.

Shaggy claps his hand over Trey's mouth. "That's enough out of you. . . . Oh, man! Did you just lick me? Gross!" He drops his hand and wipes it on his khaki pants.

"I–" Trey starts again.

But Buzz Cut has retrieved a pair of gym socks from the mess on the floor, and he stuffs them into Trey's mouth. "I'll check if the coast is clear." He peeks out the door at the back of the chapel. A second later: "We're good to go."

Shaggy's got Trey hoisted up, arms pinned back so he can't get the socks out of his mouth. He pushes the door open with his shoulder and heads out. I think Buzz will follow them, but instead he doubles back, toward me.

Oh no oh no oh no. He *did* see me, and now I'm done for.

But he just kicks at something, and the bottle sails out the door after Shaggy and Trey. Buzz follows. Then *SLAM!* goes the giant chapel door behind them.

7

In Pursuit

Once they're gone I take a second to recap what has happened so far today: I turned ten, had a party, was told I was a genie, rode a dinosaur, shrunk down and got sucked inside a bottle, popped out of another bottle and turned big again, and managed to stay out of the Reggs' line of sight.

Except they've taken my bottle with them. My bottle on the other side, that is. Uncle Max had told me quite clearly to keep it close. Having it end up in the wrong hands would be bad. Very bad indeed. Something tells me that Buzz's hands aren't the right ones. Besides that, that bottle is my ticket home, and right now home is the only place I want to be.

I scramble to my feet and move to the door, a bit unevenly with one shoe on and one shoe off. The door creaks on its hinges as I open it just a crack. There they are, at the end of a long hallway. Buzz is kicking the bottle like it's a soccer ball. "Hey, did you hear something?" Shaggy asks, and I duck back inside the chapel, quick as a wink.

Oh, man. Another close call. I need some oil or something to un-creak the hinges before I open the door again. But where would you get oil in a chapel?

Drip. Drip.

Something drips from the edge of the door onto my bare foot. I bend down and swipe at it with my fingers. Greasy and slick like snot. Ew.

Hold up. That's *oil.*

I made oil! I just thought of it, and now it's there! Holy smokes!

So the trick is, I think of things and they appear. That's not hard at all. I've got this genie thing covered, no problem.

I need that bottle back in my hands, I think.

And . . . nothing.

Shoot. What am I doing wrong? I think it again, harder: *I need that bottle back in my hands.* I add the word *wish* to my thoughts: *I wish I had that bottle back in my hands.* But still nothing.

Okay, now I'm just wasting time. There is the oiled door, at least, so I open it again. Creak-free this time. Unfortunately, Trey and the dirtballs aren't in the hall anymore. Here's what is in the hall: endless lockers, and signs up above them that say things like "Millings Academy Lacrosse: UNDEFEATED!" and "Millings Academy Yearbook Staff Meeting THIS Monday!"

Millings Academy! As in MA!

Academy is another word for school, which accounts for the backpacks, the lockers, and all of them dressed the same. They have school uniforms. That's got to be it–and it makes a lot more sense than all three of them wearing Massachusetts shirts. I mean, I think Pennsylvania is a good place to live, but I don't have a special PA shirt.

But what kind of school would have its very own chapel? And more important, why would anyone be here on a Saturday?

Am I at a college? Nah, those kids are too young for college. Unless they're geniuses or something–that's geniuses, not genies. Though judging by the three I saw so far, that doesn't seem very likely.

Whatever they are, as long as they have my bottle, I have to find them.

There are double doors at the end of the hall, so I run toward them, faster than I've ever run in my life. I'm a bit lopsided, with one shoe off and one shoe still on, but there's no time to worry about that. I push open the double doors. Outside is all bright colors. The sun is shining high in a clear blue sky. There's a field of grass so green, it looks like it was colored in that way. On the left, it's bordered by tennis courts. On the right, there are three HUGE houses made of red brick. Each house has a different sign out front: "Daly Hall," "McGuire Hall," "Food Hall."

Food Hall? Like a cafeteria? We have one of those at our school. It doesn't look a thing like this one, though. Ours is in the basement of a plain redbrick building. And we don't have tennis courts across the way, either.

Hey, I bet this is one of those fancy boarding schools, like where Quinn's friend Bella goes!

Shaggy, Buzz, and Trey are nowhere in sight. Where could they be? Where would I be if I didn't want to be caught dragging a kid to a dump? I scan the area again. There are woods beyond the tennis courts–I'd go there.

When I squint my eyes, there's a strange *click, click, click* behind my eyeballs. Suddenly I can see farther and more clearly than I've ever seen before. Like, I can see the blades of grass on the ground, and even the bark on the line of palm trees. I've never seen palm trees in person before. And if that weren't cool enough, I spot a grasshopper, resting on one single blade of grass, flicking an antenna in front of its eye.

Holy smokes, this is cool.

Focus, Zack. FOCUS. Find those kids.

Okay, I see the three of them. They *are* walking into the woods. Trey is still over Shaggy's shoulder. And Buzz has the bottle. He's tossing it high up into the air and catching it, tossing it up again, higher. Oh, he misses this time. It lands at the roots of a palm tree. I decide to wait until they've walked a bit farther. Then I'll run out and grab it. But before I can put the plan into action, Buzz swipes it from the ground and tosses it up again.

I sprint toward the woods, running as fast as Superman. *Whoosh*, I'm like the wind.

"What was that?" Buzz asks.

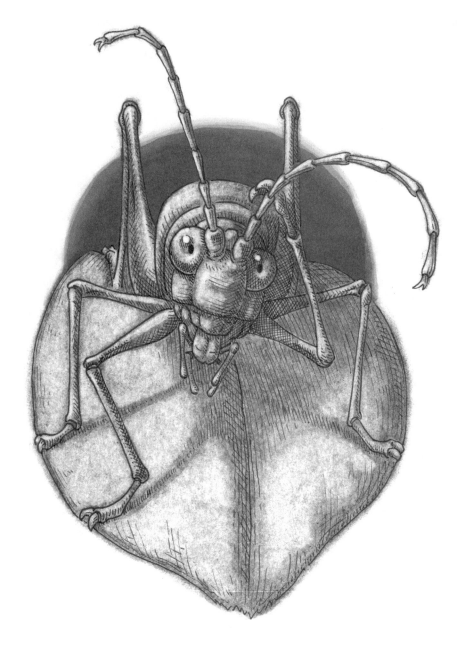

I've passed them by a few dozen yards at least, without even trying. Now I hide behind a tree, watching Buzz and Shaggy look around to make sure they're not being followed. They don't see me, and so they keep going. I creep back toward them, concentrating on moving slowly this time and staying a safe distance behind them from now on. When Shaggy stops to readjust Trey's weight on his shoulder, I duck behind a big rock. When Buzz drops the bottle–again–and turns to pick it up, I crouch by a bush.

The woods open up to an expanse of dirt and faded grass in patches. In the distance, there's a sign: "Future Home of the Twendel Athletic Center," and one of those construction site drawings showing you how beautiful and elaborate the finished product will be. I dart out and hide behind a cement mixer.

They stop at a Dumpster at the end of a gravel road. "Nice athletic center, twerp," Shaggy says sarcastically. "I'm sure you'll use it a lot, since you're such a jock and all."

Buzz puts down the bottle. Together, he and Shaggy hoist Trey into the Dumpster. "Ow!" he cries. At least he's finally been able to take the socks out of his mouth.

Shaggy bends to grab a handful of gravel and tosses it up, too. I watch the little rocks move through the air–the sunshine is pinging off them and they float in the air for a few seconds. It looks like a sparkly little galaxy, hovering right there above the Dumpster. Am I the one holding them there? With just the power of my stare?

"What the–" Buzz says, watching as the rocks are seemingly unaffected by gravity.

"Boys!" an unmistakably adult voice calls.

I blink in surprise, and the gravel drops into the Dumpster. There are *clink, clink, clink* sounds as each piece hits something unseen on the other side. But there's not another word from Trey. Not even a sigh or a grunt.

A man rushes forward. "What are you doing

down here?" he asks Shaggy and Buzz accusingly. "You have class right now!"

"We had to come down here to, ah, to throw some stuff away for Mr. Heddle," Buzz says quickly.

"Mr. Heddle, huh?" the man says. "The head of school sent *both* of you?"

"Sure did. It was especially heavy, so he needed us both." Shaggy flexes a muscle for effect. A big muscle, I might add.

"Maybe we should head to Twendel One," the man says, his voice full of fake niceness. "I'm sure Mr. Heddle will welcome you to his office, so he can personally thank you both."

"I don't think that's necessary, Mr. Gaspin," Buzz says. "It was really no problem."

"No problem at all," Shaggy adds.

"Let's go, boys," Mr. Gaspin barks.

I step one foot out from behind my hiding spot so that I can tell this guy–Mr. Gaspin–that they threw Trey into the Dumpster.

But then I step back. On second thought, if I tell him, will I get in trouble, too? Of course I didn't throw anyone into a Dumpster. But what if Mr. Gaspin gets mad at me for trespassing? It's not my fault that I'm here. But if I explain myself—*you see, I'm a genie and I came here through a bottle that's a portal*—it's not like he'll believe me, or even understand what I'm saying. What if he carts me away and I don't get the chance to grab the bottle? I will have screwed up this genie thing before I even get started, and there'd be no chance of getting home.

I don't know what to do, and before I even have time to make the decision, it's too late. They're gone.

8

Rescue #1

Mr. Gaspin and the Reggs have been gone for at least five minutes and there hasn't been a peep from inside the Dumpster. I can't even hear Trey breathing. Either he's holding his breath or . . .

Or he's dead. A handful of gravel shouldn't do that much damage. But I guess if even a tiny piece hit you in the exact right spot on your temple, you'd be a goner.

Or maybe Trey isn't dead. Maybe he's just unconscious and it's up to me to resuscitate him. I know how to do it because I looked it up on YouTube: I'll have to put my mouth on his mouth–kind of gross, but hey, I'm saving a life. Then I'll pump my hands up and down on his chest and count as I go.

Climbing into the Dumpster isn't the easiest thing in the world, especially with just one

sneaker. But my feet find the grooves on the side. I swing one leg over, then the other.

Oooph. I land on a pile of junk *and* Trey.

"OWWWWWW!" he says.

"You're alive!"

"Of course I'm alive," he says, pushing me off. Now there's something digging into my side. "But thanks to you I have a few *more* bruises."

I twist around to get comfortable–or as comfortable as one can get on a pile of metal and wooden construction scraps. "Sorry," I say.

"I thought genies were supposed to fix problems, not cause them. You sure don't act like a genie." He adjusts the broken glasses on his face. Aside from the smashed right lens, the left side of the frame is sticking up at a funny angle. "And you sure don't look like one, either."

I look down at myself–besides the missing shoe, my jeans are torn at the left knee, and there's dirt on my hands and elbows. Probably on my face, too. I push my hair out of my face.

"My mom says I look better when you can see my eyes," I say.

"Your mom? Genies have moms?"

"Oh yeah," I say. "Genies have whole families—moms, sisters, and . . ." My voice trails off.

"It doesn't matter," Trey says. "All that matters is you're a genie and I have some wishes to make, and I don't want to waste any more time, now that it finally worked."

"What finally worked?"

"Rubbing the bottle," he says. He has a look on his face like, *Duh, genie!* "All this time, I thought it had to be a fake. Just a dumb souvenir my dad brought back from his business trip to Bolivia. Or actually that his assistant brought back. My dad is too busy to waste any time shopping for me."

"So you rubbed it today?" I ask. "In the chapel?"

"I rubbed it a thousand times before today and nothing happened," he tells me. "I only had it with me today because I was going to throw it away. Then those kids showed up. And finally you popped out. Not that you were much help."

"Yeah, those guys," I say. "They seemed pretty mad at you. You must've–"

But Trey cuts me off. "Never mind them. I have *wishes* to make!" My toe tingles with the mention of that word–*wishes*. "The genies in the movies always grant wishes. I get wishes too, right?"

"Uh-huh," I say. I reach down and scratch my toe. It's pretty dirty from walking all the way from the chapel to the construction site. You can't even see my birthmark anymore. I scrap off some dust and mud with my fingernails. Then I pick the dirt out from under my nails and flick it away.

Trey scoots back, even though I wasn't flicking the dirt anywhere near him–honest. "The genies in the movies are not at all this gross," he says.

"Hollywood got a few things wrong," I explain.

"Clearly," Trey says. "Is wearing just one shoe a genie thing?"

"I don't think so," I tell him. "But I only found out today that I'm a genie."

"Ugh," he says. "A newbie? I got a newbie?" He's shaking his head. "No wonder I'm in a Dumpster. Patricia should've picked a bottle with a genie that actually knows what he's doing."

"I'm doing my best," I say. "I climbed in here after you, even though I didn't have to. I only did it to be nice and helpful. And you could've made it easier. Like, you could've popped your head up or waved your arm or shouted or *something* when they left, just to let me know you weren't dead."

"It's not my job to do you any favors."

"Or you could've said something when that teacher came around," I say.

Trey's chin drops, just slightly, but I know I'm onto something.

"That guy, Mr Gaspin, he would've helped you out for sure," I go on. "And it's not like you

108

knew I'd be waiting here to rescue you. Unless . . . unless you were afraid they'd get you even worse next time, if you ratted them out. That's it, huh?"

"I'm not afraid of them," Trey says, folding his arms across his chest. "I'm not afraid of anyone."

"Yeah, right," I say.

"Yeah," he says. "Right. They only do that stuff to me because they're afraid of *me*."

"They didn't look so afraid," I tell him.

"Trust me," he says. "They're terrified. You should be, too. Do you know who I am?"

"We weren't formally introduced," I remind him. "But I know your name is Trey."

"I'm pretty sure that you're supposed to call me Master."

And that would make me his servant? Uh-uh. No way. No how. If he thinks that, he has another think coming.

"Maybe I should just call you twerp," I say.

"I wouldn't if I were you. Trey is short for

Preston Hudson Twendel the third." He pulls a plastic card out of his pocket and flashes it in front of my face.

"What's that?"

"My key card to my dorm," he says. "It has my name and my picture–see?" He flashes it again.

"Twendel," I say. "That name sounds familiar."

He shifts his weight and stuffs the card back in his pocket. "It's the name of this construction site we're on right now," he tells me. "My grandfather was Preston Hudson Twendel the first, and my dad is the second. You know who *they* are, right?"

"Am I supposed to?"

"Everyone does," he says. "My grandfather is the guy who started PHT Capital, which happens to be the biggest bank in the world."

"Huh," I say. "My mom has an account there."

"Of course she does," Trey says. "And my dad is the president of the whole thing. When I grow up, it'll be MY bank. So what do you have to say to that?"

I shrug. "That's cool for you and your dad," I say.

"That's right," he says. "It is. Money makes you powerful."

I remember that Uncle Max said being a genie does, too. If only I could figure out how to make that work in my favor!

"My dad has more money than anyone," Trey goes on. "He basically owns Millings Academy. It's the best boarding school in all of California."

Hold up. Did he say California? I'm in *California*? That's clear across the country from Pennsylvania!

"If my dad wanted to, he could get Oliver and Jake kicked out." I know he means Shaggy and Buzz. "He could get them kicked out like that." Trey snaps his fingers. "My dad doesn't tolerate losers. He just gets rid of them. If he knew those two losers threw me in a Dumpster, he'd get rid of them for sure." He pauses, for just a second. "And then he'd get rid of me for being the loser who let them."

"So you *are* afraid of someone," I say. "Your dad."

"Maybe I am. But I bet you're afraid of *your* dad."

"He's dead," I say quickly. I've learned that's the best way to say those words, like you're ripping off a Band-Aid. It hurts, but then it's over with.

For a split second there's a flash of panic in Trey's eyes, the same look everyone gets when they first hear. After that, they either become really curious and want me to tell them all the sad and scary details, or they want to get away from me as fast as possible, like having a dead father is catching or something.

But Trey recovers quickly. "So are you going to do any magic, or do I have to get out of here myself?"

"Uh," I start.

"Never mind, newbie. We'll just climb out." Trey stands and reaches up toward the top of the Dumpster. "I'll go first. You spot me from this side. It's the least you can do." He stands up and holds on to the side of the Dumpster, looking over his shoulder at me. "You're lucky anyway, about not having a dad," he says. "I might have you get rid of mine."

"I wouldn't get rid of anyone's dad," I tell him.

"I think you have to do whatever I tell you. And just so you know, my dad's not a good person. He's not even a good dad. Every single teacher here sucks up to him. Gaspin would've reported straight to him if he'd found me here. The trouble Oliver and Jake are going to be in is nothing compared to what I would've faced. So, about my first wish."

Oh no. Something's happening. My toe is itching and burning. What if he makes the wish to get rid of his dad? And what if I can't control myself, and I accidentally grant it?

"I wish," he starts.

All right, Zack, it's time to think outside the bottle!

Ooh, the bottle–that's it!

"Hold up," I tell Preston Hudson Twendel III. "Those kids left the bottle on the ground, and I need it before I do any wish granting."

I don't, really. At least I don't think I do. But this twerp doesn't know that, and I have a plan: (1) get out of the Dumpster; (2) grab the bottle; (3) run as far away as possible; (4) get sucked up and get home.

I'm not sure how to make the getting-home part happen, but I'll deal with that after I've completed the first three parts of the plan.

Trey is out of the Dumpster now, so it's my turn. One foot over, then another, and now a jump down to the ground. Oomph.

But when I stand up and wipe the dirt off myself, the bottle is nowhere in sight. "Where is it?" I ask.

"The bottle? I don't see it. Does this mean I don't get my wishes? That is SO UNFAIR!"

9

Why Me?

We have no choice but to head back toward the school buildings in search of the bottle. I take off my remaining shoe, because it's easier to walk when my feet feel more balanced, and follow Trey as he mutters complaints about getting stuck with me–the worst genie in the world. I don't know how he knows that. I mean, sure, there's room for improvement. But how many other genies has Trey ever met? And better ones, at that? I'm willing to bet the answer is exactly zero.

Trey is kicking at the ground as he walks, sending sprays of dust and rocks into the air.

Every so often I pause to stare at them, trying to get them to hover in the air like a galaxy, the way they did before. But the magic seems to be gone. Above us, the clouds start to thicken and send shadows across the vast lawn and large buildings of Millings Academy. I wonder if a thunderstorm is coming. Thunderstorms often mean lightning. Each year an average of fifty-one people are killed by lightning strikes in the United States. It's especially dangerous to be outside in an open field, which we happen to be in right now. "Let's go faster," I tell Trey.

"You're the genie, and I'm the master," he replies. "We'll go as fast as I want."

He slows his pace so he's traveling at the speed limit of your average snail. "Fine," I say. "But the longer it takes to get there, the longer it takes to get the bottle, and the longer it takes–"

I don't even have to finish my sentence before Trey starts taking giant strides. But then there's a rumble of thunder in the distance, and

I drop to the ground and flatten myself like a pancake.

"What are you doing?" Trey asks.

I cock my head to listen. Where there's one roll of thunder, there are usually more. But now the only sound is Trey's heavy, impatient breathing.

"Get up," he says, and I do. We finally make it across the field to a building with the words TWENDEL HALL II carved out above an imposing red door.

"Aren't you going to open it for me?" Trey asks.

Uncle Max didn't tell me that being a genie would feel so much like being a servant. I wonder what I did to deserve this. Why is this happening to me? Why did I have to be born with a genie bite? Why did my bottle have to end up in the hands of the worst kid in the world? (If he gets to call me the worst genie, then I get to call him the worst kid. And you know what? Even if

I haven't met all the other kids in the world to form that conclusion, I think I'm probably pretty close to the mark.) Why did he have to rub it and summon me on my very first day on the job?

Why do bad things always happen to *me*?

My limbs feel suddenly heavier. Not that Trey cares. "I'm waiting," he says.

I let out the world's biggest sigh and pull open the door. Trey goes inside and I scoot in after him. At least this building is safer than an open field. Plus, I don't know my way around Millings Academy. Which means I have a better chance of finding that bottle with Trey than without him.

I'm stuck with him, which may be the most depressing thing of all.

I wish I could turn back into the kid I was just this morning. Sure, I didn't have many friends to invite to my birthday party or a pile of presents to show for it. But, boy, do I miss being in my old, boring life.

We've stepped into a room that's so big, I think you could probably fit my entire house inside it. It's way fancier than my house–fancier than any house I've ever been in. It's fancy enough to be a hotel lobby, or maybe the lobby of a museum. The windows have deep-rose-colored drapes tied back with matching rope tassels. The bottoms of the drapes brush the floor, which is black-and-white checkerboard marble. Gold chandeliers hang from the ceiling. The ceiling itself is like looking up at the sky. Really– it's sky blue with clouds that seem to pop off like they were painted in 3-D. The walls are painted maroon, a shade darker than the drapes, and on the far wall there's a huge oil painting of a stern-faced old man. It's framed in the same dark gold color as the chandeliers. I step closer to it and see the matching gold plaque under the painting: P. H. TWENDEL.

"That's my grandfather," Trey tells me. "He commissioned this building for Millings

Academy."

"I don't know what 'commissioned' means," I admit.

"What *do* you know?" Trey says with an eye roll. It's the kind of question I know I'm not meant to answer. "It means he paid for it to be built."

Holy smokes, how rich would you have to be to build a building like this?

"I'm sure he wouldn't want a useless newbie genie staring at his portrait," Trey says. "Come on."

I follow him out of the room and down a long hallway. It's carpeted, and it feels good under my bare feet, extra soft and extra thick. It's definitely the softest, thickest carpeting I've ever walked on. Back at home, the carpet is kind of old and worn thin. And at my school, we don't have carpet at all. The floors are plain old scratched-up linoleum, and–

BRRRIIIINNNNGGGG!!!! goes the world's loudest bell.

Is the hallway on fire? Is the *building* on fire?

Those lobby drapes looked awfully flammable.

"Quick, in here," Trey says, pushing open a door. There's a sign on it that says, "Under Construction: No Entry."

In the background, there's a stampede of footsteps.

My heart is pounding at least as hard. "Nearly three thousand people have died in construction-site accidents in the last twenty-five years," I say in a rush. "We don't even have hard hats."

Trey doesn't say another word. He just grabs my arm and pulls me in with him.

On the other side of the door there's . . .

A bathroom.

A really fancy one, of course. The floor is made of sparkly tiles. There are three wooden stall doors that go all the way to the ground, so you can't peek under them and see who's in there. Plus, three sinks. They're not hooked up to the walls yet, and the drains are coming out of the wall behind them. There's also a big gold mirror waiting to be hung.

"I don't think anyone's supposed to be in here," I say.

"Precisely," Trey says. "I came in here because no one else will. You need a private place to come up with a plan to get that bottle back. And I need a private place to think of what wishes to make."

With the mention of the W-word, my big toe wakes up and starts tingling again.

Trey pushes his crooked glasses up the bridge of his nose. The left side sticks up at an even higher angle. "Maybe I'll wish for Jake and Oliver to come down with a mystery illness that makes them puke for seven straight days," he says.

My stomach twists at the thought of puking for that long.

"Or maybe," he goes on, "I'll wish that no one will be allowed to step into any building that anyone in my family paid to build unless they have my permission—and if they want my permission, they'll have to do some serious sucking up to get it. Or maybe I'll wish . . ."

Trey's still talking. Meanwhile, my foot's still itching. The worst spot is right on the genie bite. It's traveling down the line of my toes. I reach down, trying to be oh-so-casual about it, and scratch and scratch. Ooh, that's better.

"What is it with you and your foot?" Trey asks.

"It's an old genie ritual to formulate a plan to find one's bottle," I tell him. "Scratch your toes and the answer will come to you."

Trey's mouth twists like he's just sucked on a lemon. "The answers better come fast," he says. I keep on scratching, even though it's not making the itching go away. Trey pushes open the heavy wooden door of the stall on the far right. "If my dad saw they'd used oak on these doors instead of walnut, he'd have a fit."

"They seem fine to me," I tell him. "Did your family pay for all this, too?"

"Affirmative," Trey says.

I've never heard anyone say that word before, but I know without asking that it means yes.

"Jake and Ollie are probably still in Heddle's office," he says.

"Heddle is the head of the school?" I ask. Trey nods. "Is that the same as a principal?"

"Yup," Trey says. "And I can think of some wishes about getting rid of him, too."

Itch. Itch. Itch.

"Once we get the bottle back, if Heddle gives us any trouble or tries to call my dad, I'll just wish him away. I'll wish them all away." Trey pauses, and looks over at me. "What do you think about that plan?"

Scratch. Scratch. Scratch.

"I'm still thinking," I tell him.

"While you're thinking, I'm going to go to the bathroom." Trey pauses before ducking into the stall. "It's a shame for Jake and Ollie. It's a shame for all the kids at Millings. None of them like me very much, and I'm the one with all of the wishes."

Trey takes a deep breath, and then so soft it's almost to himself, he adds, "Actually, here's my wish. I wish I could turn into someone people like."

There's a sound, like a snap. I guess it's the stall door clicking shut, though I've never heard a door sound like that before. But never mind that. Right now my whole foot is itching so badly, it's as if I stuck it in a tank of mosquitoes that hadn't had anything to eat for a week. I shake it all about, like I'm playing the hokey pokey, which at ten years old, I am way too old to play.

Ten years old! I remember being home at my birthday party just a few hours ago, leaning over the cake. I had a wish of my own, and to tell you the truth, it wasn't so different than the wish Trey just made. Just before I blew out my half of the candles, I said in my head: *I wish next year on my eleventh birthday, I have a crowd of friends watching. Even more friends than Quinn.*

But I don't care about my wish right now—
or Trey's, either. My foot is practically on fire. If I
were blowing candles out now, I'd wish to make
it stop.

I don't have any calamine lotion with me,
but there are three sinks here. Ice-cold water on
my foot would feel mighty good right about now.

I hop over—my foot's too itchy to walk on—
and turn the dial. The pipes make a gurgling
sound. I turn the dial around a bit more. No
gurgling this time. Hmmm. Now what?

I'm about to turn around, thinking maybe
I'll stick my foot in the toilet water. Quinn would
think that's the grossest thing I've ever done, but
everything in this bathroom is brand-new, never
used before. And besides, desperate times call for
desperate measures.

Gurgle, gurgle goes the sink, and then
SPLASH! The water comes out in a rush all at
once. I twist the knob to turn it off. Water has

splattered all down the front of my shirt and dripped down to my pants and my bare feet.

I look in the mirror to assess the damage, and when I catch my reflection, my hair looks so . . . so neat.

Kinda like the way Uncle Max's hair had looked when he was performing his own magic.

Uh-oh.

I hear Trey unlatch the stall door. He pulls it toward himself and steps out, one brown loafer at a time.

Holy smokes. That's not Trey.

That's Quinn.

10

OH, THE QUINNSANITY

My mouth is open but I've forgotten how to make words come out. If I could speak, I would say: Oh, the *quinnsanity*!

Quinnsanity. Noun. Insanity that involves Quinn.

Quinn, meanwhile, isn't having a problem talking, and her words come out in a rush.

"Where am I?" she asks. "Where's Madeline? What is this place? And why are these things on my face?" She knocks Trey's glasses to the floor. The remaining unsmashed lens now smashes, too, making the glasses completely useless. Quinn looks down. "Why am I wearing these . . . these *clothes*?!"

Clothes are important to Quinn. She takes about an hour to choose an outfit in the morning, and usually goes through several "test" outfits before settling on the one she's actually going to wear for the day. But now she is dressed in nothing she'd ever pick out for herself: khaki pants, a green-collared MA shirt, thick white socks, and brown loafers.

There's something else strange about her, and it takes me a second to realize it's her hair. It's parted down the middle with the left half up in some kind of braid, and the right half hanging loose across her shoulder.

But I still can't get any words out, and she's not done speaking anyway.

"Zack? ZACK? ZACHARY NOAH COOLEY, I'M GOING TO TELL MOM ON YOU AND YOU'RE GOING TO BE IN SO MUCH TROUBLE!"

"I . . . I . . . ," I stutter. I move past her and glance into the stall she just came out of, looking for Trey. But he's not in there. Not that I expected him to be. In fact, I suspect I know what's going on, but my suspicion is insane, and out of this world. It's absolutely, positively the most crazmazingest thing I've ever suspected before.

For just a second, the bathroom is silent, except for the slightest *gurgle, gurgle* from the sink. Quinn puts her hands on her hips. "You have three seconds before I start to scream. Three. Two. O–"

"All right. All right. I was at Uncle Max's and he gave me a bottle and–" I stop short. "The problem is, if I just tell you flat out what happened today–that I learned I'm a genie–you're not going to understand me."

"What?" she asks.

"I tried to tell you before," I say. "It's not my fault the words don't make sense. It's a safety mechanism the board put in place."

"A safety mechanism? From the board?" Quinn repeats. She's shaking her head. "You're right you're not making any sense. And hey, genius, if you're a genie, where's your bottle, then?"

"The Reggs took it with them," I say. But then I cut myself off. "Wait, you understand me?"

"I understand you're a nut job and a liar." Her eyes scan the room and I can practically see the wheels turning in her head, trying to figure out where she is and how I managed to get her here.

But there's something *I* just figured out. "Holy smokes! I just discovered an exception to Genie Board Decision two hundred and fifty-eight!"

"Zack!" Quinn says. "Tell me what's really going on here!"

"I *am* telling you," I say. "It's supposed to come out like gibberish when I talk about genie stuff. That's what Uncle Max said. But I can tell Trey, of course, since he's the one who rubbed the bottle. And if he makes a wish and I turn him into you–"

"Who the heck is Trey?"

"The one who made the wish that brought you here," I tell her. "You turned into him. Well, sort of. It's you, but you're wearing his clothes."

"You expect me to believe that this kid, this Trey–someone I've never met–made a wish to become me?"

"Not exactly," I say. "He wished to turn into someone people liked. And you popped into my head because, well . . ." I toe the ground, feeling a little embarrassed. I may be a genie, but I don't know how to be popular, like Quinn does. "People like you," I mumble.

"That's right, they do," Quinn says. "Unlike some people I know."

"Don't get such a big head about it," I say. "I don't think Trey would actually like *being* you. But at least it helped me discover the exception. So I can talk about being a genie and you'll understand."

"I understand that you need serious help,"

Quinn says. "Mom will probably send you to a mental hospital when I tell her."

"She will not," I say. But really I'm not so sure. After all, I was convinced Uncle Max had Alzheimer's disease when he first told me. And explaining things to Mom might be impossible with Genie Board Decision 258 in place. Unless there's a *second* exception to the rule, in the event your mom is about to have you committed. I'll have to ask Uncle Max about that–if I ever see him again. Which reminds me, I have bigger problems right now.

"You know what else I think?" Quinn asks, and she keeps on talking without waiting for my answer. "I think there was another pair of twins being born at Pinemont Hospital on this exact day, ten years ago, and you got switched out with my real brother." She's nodding to herself now. "Yeah, that's it. We're not really related after all!"

"Wishful thinking," I mutter.

"I know you love to play make-believe and

pretend to swoop in and rescue people, but you've gone too far this time."

"I'm telling the truth, and I can prove it to you."

"Oh, really? How?"

"Isn't being here proof enough?"

"I don't know where *here* is!" she says.

"This is Millings Academy," I tell her. "In *California*."

"Yeah, right."

"Fine, if you don't believe me, I'll prove it another way."

Uncle Max had licked his finger and twirled it in the air. So I do that, but nothing happens. There's certainly no car-horse-zebra-dinosaur combination.

"This is ridiculous," Quinn says.

"Okay, look," I say. "See those sinks on the floor, and how their pipes aren't hooked up?" Quinn nods. "Well, I made water come out of them! Just before you got here–I turned the faucet and the water rushed out. Here, watch."

I twist the dial on the same sink I used before, but nothing. I try the knobs on the other two, but their spouts remain dry.

"Nice try," Quinn says.

"No, really," I say. "Look–I'm all wet from before–the water just came rushing out and–" But even as I say it, I realize my shirt and my pants and my feet are bone-dry, like I really had made the whole thing up. "Maybe genies can't get wet," I tell her.

"I don't have time for this stupid game," Quinn says. Her voice is shaky. I think she may even start to cry. "Madeline was in the middle of braiding my hair. She's waiting for me. I've GOT TO GET HOME!"

"Don't worry, I have an idea." How come I didn't think of this already? "Just make a wish saying you want to go back to who you were before."

"I want to be who I was before," Quinn says. Nothing.

"It's not working because you were Quinn before, and you're still you. You need to say you want to be Trey again. And say 'I wish.' "

Quinn folds her arms across her chest, like she really doesn't want to be bothered saying it, but she does–probably because even if she thinks I'm a nut job, she still hasn't figured out how I got her into this bathroom in the first place. "I *wish* I were Trey again." She waits for about the amount of time it takes a hummingbird to flap its wings. "Nope. Didn't work."

"Go into the bathroom stall and come out again," I say. "That's what worked last time."

Quinn turns around and heads into the same exact stall as before. The stall where the magic happens. But as soon as the oak door closes, my heart starts to pound. After all, I don't know where Trey disappeared to when Quinn popped up in his place. And I don't know where Quinn will be going now. Maybe home.

But maybe not.

Maybe she'll disappear FOREVER!

"Quinn!" I shout.

"Yeah, nut job," she says.

"Oh, thank goodness," I say.

She opens the stall door and steps back out. "What do you have to be thankful for?"

I can't tell her the answer. Instead, I stare down at my big toe, at my genie bite. The one I inherited from Uncle Max. "Let's call Uncle Max," I tell Quinn.

Another thing I can't believe I didn't think of. I'll call Uncle Max, and he'll come here and do whatever genie tricks need to be done to get it all sorted out.

"So we need a phone," Quinn says. "I don't have one and neither do you, since Mom won't let us get cell phones."

"But I know just where to find one."

11

Going to the Chapel

I push open the bathroom door extra slowly and peek out into the hall to make sure it's empty. Then I motion for Quinn to follow. "Where are we going?" she asks.

"We have to retrace my steps back to the chapel," I tell her. "That's where Trey's cell phone is."

"His cell phone is in a chapel?"

"It fell out of his backpack, and it's lying on the floor." I silently scold myself for not grabbing it up when I had the chance.

"Why didn't he pick it up?"

"It's a long story," I say. "Come on."

I tiptoe down the hall. Quinn is following me, but apparently she didn't get the memo that we're supposed to be acting stealthy. Nope, she's walking down the middle of the hall like she thinks she owns it, and she's jabbering away: "I must be dreaming. That's the only logical explanation. Madeline went home, and I had dinner and went to bed. I don't remember those things, but they must've happened, and now I'm fast asleep." She lifts her left arm and pinches the skin with her right fingers. "Okay, I felt that. But maybe that's just a rumor, that you can't feel anything in your dreams. It's not like we can really prove it."

"Can't you be quiet for once?" I hiss.

"It doesn't matter if anyone hears me if I'm dreaming," Quinn says, even louder.

"You're *not* dreaming," I say. My voice is barely a whisper. "You're just in the denial stage."

Uncle Max said there was a denial stage for finding out you're a genie. Apparently there's also one for finding out about your genie brother.

At the end of the hall I glance around the corner to make sure no one is there. When I'm sure the coast is clear, I make a mad dash for the lobby.

But Quinn is just standing there taking it all in—the checkerboard floor and chandeliers, the maroon walls and the oil paintings in gilded frames. "Whoa."

"Come on," I tell her. "Come *on*."

I've already crossed the room and pushed open the front door. Quinn comes over and steps outside. Her eyes skim the expanse of lawn in front of us, perfectly groomed, the palm trees lining the borders, and the huge redbrick buildings. Above us the clouds are light gray, but they look heavier in the distance. Quinn, of course, isn't worried about them.

"California, did you say?" she asks, and I nod. "It's always been my dream to go to California. But in real life I would pick someone else to travel with."

"Yeah, well, me too," I tell her. "Anyway, that way is the under-construction athletic center." I point as I remember. "And to get back to the chapel we have to . . ." It's hard to retrace your steps when you made a stop in between them, but I don't want to go all the way back to the Dumpster first, because that would mean having to spend even more time outside. "I think we go that way." I turn around in a circle, trying to figure it out. "I need a map," I say to myself. And just like that, there on the limestone sidewalk, the different buildings and pathways are carved out and glittering, like stars in the sky.

"Holy smokes! Look what I made!"

Quinn is barely impressed, until she notices one building on the map, the one labeled "Food Hall."

"I'm so hungry," she says. "I can't remember ever being hungry in my sleep before. Maybe I went to bed without eating dinner." She pauses. "At least I don't remember having dinner."

"Because you haven't had dinner yet," I tell her.

If not for this whole genie thing, Uncle Max probably would've made cheeseburgers for him and me. He has a very special way of making them–he chops up the cheese and puts it *inside* the burger part. It's actually quite genius.

That's genius, and NOT genie.

I could eat five Max burgers in one sitting– even if I wasn't hungry. They're just that good. And thinking of them makes me VERY hungry. But I shake my head. We cannot go to Food Hall. There is no time for a pit stop right now. "We've got to get to the chapel and grab Trey's phone and call Uncle Max."

"Can you stop it with that story already? This is ONLY a dream–and since it's MY dream, Food Hall must have all my favorites."

It's annoying how Quinn can't get it through her head that this genie thing is real, but I guess it's *dumberstandable*.

Dumberstandable. Adjective. When someone is behaving in a dumb, and yet somewhat understandable, way.

Quinn starts marching up the pathway toward Food Hall. The chapel is just a few yards away. There's no sign out front like the other buildings, but there is a large stained glass window on the side, so I know it's the right place. I grab Quinn's arm. Which is, of course, the exact wrong thing to do, because before I even know what's happening, she's holding *my* arm behind my back.

But I arch my back and twist free. It's the first time I've ever been able to break out of Quinn's grip.

"Whoa," she says, shaking out her hand. "You've never been . . . that powerful." She's clenching and unclenching her hand. "Actually, I can't make my fist as tight as I usually can."

"Come on," I say. "Let's get Trey's phone. The chapel isn't far."

We sprint together, but when we get there, I pull open the door extra slowly and peek my head around. "The coast is clear," I tell my sister.

We step inside. I'm about to head to the aisle, just left of the pews, where the backpack and all of Trey's stuff had been. But Quinn has stopped in her tracks. "Whoa," she says softly. "It looks just like . . . you know, it looks like . . . where we had Dad's . . ."

"I know," I say. "But come on, the phone was right over here."

Except now the aisle where Trey's stuff had been strewn about is totally clear. I walk down the length of it to make sure. But there isn't so much as a rubbed-down eraser on the floor.

"Where's the phone?" Quinn asks.

"It's gone," I say. I hear a rustling noise coming from behind a back door I hadn't noticed before. "Quick, Quinn!" I say. "Duck for cover!"

"What?"

There's more rustling. When I look toward

the door, I see the knob turning, turning.

"Between the pews, and fast!"

But while I nose-dive toward the navy-blue cushions, Quinn just stands there like a deer in headlights. I hear the door open, and the *clomp, clomp, clomp* of heavy footsteps. From my vantage point on the ground, I spy a man wearing the same MA shirt as the Reggs and Trey (I mean, Quinn). Except this guy's shirt must be size XXXL. He's the biggest man I've ever seen. He's holding a broom in one hand and a big black garbage bag in the other.

"Zack," my sister says, glancing down at me, and I can't tell if she's nervous or just irritated.

"No, I'm not Zack," the man says. His voice is deep and gravelly.

"Sorry, I was talking to my brother."

"You visiting him?" the man asks.

"I guess you could say that," Quinn says. "But he's hiding." With her thumb, she points to me lying beneath a pew.

"Hiding, huh?"

No use in hiding now. I come out from under the pew. I have to tip up my chin to see the top of this guy's head. He has to be at least nine feet tall. Or maybe ten feet tall. Double-digits height!

"Shouldn't your brother be in class?"

"Class? On a Saturday?"

"There's class every Saturday at Millings Academy," he says. "Your brother never told you that?"

"No, but he doesn't go here, exactly."

"What exactly does he do?"

"We have to go," I say. "Now."

"Wait," Quinn says to me. She looks back up—way up—at the man. "Can I ask you something?" The man nods. "Well, we were looking for a cell phone. My brother said this kid Trey left his on the floor in here—don't ask me why he did, but that's what Zack said. Anyway, I wondered if you'd picked it up. Or maybe swept it up, and it's in that garbage bag you're holding."

"I don't know what the rules are at whatever school you attend, missy," the man says. "But here at Millings Academy, we don't encourage people to take property that belongs to others." He reaches an arm as thick as a leg toward Quinn. "I think you better come with me."

"Uh, Zack," Quinn says.

"Zack?" the man repeats.

"Never mind," I say. "We don't want anyone else's property."

I try to pull Quinn out of the man's grasp with my superhuman genie strength. But it seems right now all I have is regular Zack strength. (Or, more accurately, regular Zack lack of strength.)

My heart feels like it's knocking around in my chest, and my brain hurts trying to think of a way to get us out of this.

Think, Zack. THINK!

If only there was a way to knock the giant off his feet, then he'd drop Quinn's arm and she could get away . . . Wait a second. Maybe there is! This morning I'd made a shoving motion with my hands, and Quinn had been knocked to the ground.

I do it again. And again, and again. But it's not working, and time is running out. He's twisting around and pulling Quinn with him.

And then, from behind the man's big basketball head, I notice a bumblebee flying toward us. My eyes do their click-click thing. I can see the bee's yellow and black stripes as clear as if they're under a microscope, and I can see, tucked between little fibers of hair on its legs, wads of pollen.

I'm allergic to pollen, and all of a sudden I feel a heaviness in the back of my eyes. They squeeze shut involuntarily, and from the deepest part of my chest comes the biggest, loudest sneeze of my whole entire life. Ahhhh ahhhh ahhhh AHHHH AHHHH CHOOOOOOOOOOOOOOO!

There's a sound like the wind in a category-five tornado. When I open my eyes, the man is flying across the chapel. *CRASH!* He smashes against the back wall, and a potted plant falls on his head.

Quinn herself is fine. She's standing there, right next to me. I guess she wasn't in the path of the tornado–er, the sneeze.

There's no time to waste. I grab her hand and call, "Sorry," over my shoulder. It's not like I wanted to hurt the guy, after all. Seconds later we're out the door and hiding around the corner of the building. I pull Quinn behind a tree, which frankly, isn't that much bigger than the man. We are both huffing and puffing a bit from running so fast, but Quinn is huffing and puffing an extra amount. In my head I see Drew Listerman in the television studio. "That was amazing, Zack." And I see everyone at home watching their TVs, nodding: amazing.

But when Quinn finally catches her breath, does she tell me I was amazing, or say thank you, or anything like that? Nope. She rubs her arms and says, "Ew, Zack, you spit on me!"

"I *saved* you," I tell her.

Not that Quinn can give me credit for anything. "Yeah, well, now what?"

I'm about to admit that I don't know, when suddenly, it comes to me. "How do you talk to Bella on the phone?" I ask.

"We don't talk on the phone," she says. "We Skype."

"Exactly."

"So?" my sister asks. "What good does that do us now? Do you have a computer in your pocket?"

"No, but check yours."

"You think I have a computer in *my* pocket?" She's rolling her eyes as she reaches in and pulls out a white piece of plastic in the shape of a credit card. "Huh. I don't know what this is."

"Quinn," I say. "It's a key."

12

FOOD HALL

"Trey showed me the key before," I explain to Quinn. "It's to his dorm room—to *your* dorm room."

"I don't have a dorm room," she says. "Just a regular bedroom in our regular house. Though I wouldn't mind having a dorm room right now. If I went to school with Bella, I wouldn't have to see you!"

"Listen, Quinn," I say sternly. "We don't have time to go over and over and over this. *You* are Trey now. You have a dorm room. And I'm willing to bet that dorm room has a computer in it. So if we go there, we can log on, call Uncle Max, and get everything fixed."

"All right," she says.

"All right?"

"Sure. Lead the way."

"Hang on." I turn in a circle again, to make the glittering map reappear. But the sidewalk stays a plain, ordinary sidewalk.

"Some genie you are," Quinn says.

"Like you could do any better if you were a genie."

"I totally could," she says. "But I wouldn't want to be one."

I don't want to, either, but I can't get into all that. "I guess we can go around to every building and test the doors. But that'll take a long time."

"Ugh, I'm SO TIRED," Quinn says. She yawns for dramatic effect. But she does look a bit more glassy-eyed than usual. "I have a better idea—a faster idea. Let's *ask* someone."

She steps out from behind the building and

starts walking. "I don't know," I say, hanging back.

"Your plan takes too long. You said that yourself. Plus, it looks like it's going to rain, and I don't want to get my hair wet as we race from building to building."

Not that I care about Quinn's hair, but she's right about my way taking too long. I don't want to be running around outside in a thunderstorm. "Okay," I agree. "We'll find someone to ask. But I think there should be a few rules—no asking adults. You don't want the wrong teacher wondering what you're doing here visiting on a Saturday instead of a Sunday, or thinking we're going to steal from Trey. Or thinking—"

"Stop worrying so much."

"Quinn, I'm serious. We could be sent to the police."

"Fine, I'll ask a kid."

"A kid," I repeat. "But a nice-looking one."

Quinn presses forward, toward Food Hall.

No surprise that that's where she figures we'll find the right kid to ask. Inside there's a short hallway that opens up into a MASSIVE dining hall. A digital sign proclaims, "Today's Specials: Three-Cheese Lasagna! Make Your Own Tacos! Full Salad Bar! Do-It-Yourself Ice-Cream Sundaes!"

The tables are empty. Farther down a few adults are setting up food stations for whenever the next meal is. I see taco shells being lined up, and a salad bar with all the fixings still covered in plastic. There's a freezer section and I don't have to peek to know that if you lifted the lid, you'd find ice cream in every flavor.

"They really do have all my faves," Quinn says. "Let's eat!"

I shake my head. "We can't take food before it's mealtime," I tell her. "That's asking for trouble."

"So just levitate the food over to us, *genie*."

"The Food Hall workers would notice levitating food for sure," I say. "Besides, I don't know how to make my powers come out like that."

Quinn leans against the wall and closes her eyes for a few seconds. I can't tell if she doesn't want to look at me anymore, or if she's just thinking.

She opens them again. "You know you can send people flying with a sneeze," she says. I nod. "So if one of them sees us and gets angry, you can just give 'em one of those supersonic sneezes, and we'll run out."

"I can't just sneeze on command."

Quinn reaches out and lightly runs a finger above my upper lip, just under my nose. *Ahh Ahh Ahh* . . . She pulls it away just before the sneeze comes out. "If we need a sneeze, we'll make it happen," she says. "Come on."

I glance across the room. The thing is, the lasagna *does* smell delicious. From a distance it looks delicious, too. And when I look back at Quinn, she seems a little pale. Maybe food would be a good idea for us both.

"Okay, fine. I'll go–alone." I can't risk Quinn going out there, too. What if the tornado sneeze sends her flying this time? "If I need to sneeze, I'll tickle my own nose."

"So let me tell you what I want . . ."

I'm not really listening because I'm looking at the Food Hall workers, two women and one man bent over platters. And I'm looking at all the places to hide behind along the way–I can run and then duck under a table. I can go a little farther and duck under another. And then crouch by the wall. And then hide behind the freezer.

It's good to have the Sneeze Plan as Plan B. But Plan A is to not get caught at all.

"GO!" Quinn says. She pushes me out. My heart is pounding as I dart to a table and crouch down, dart and crouch down, dart and crouch, until I've crossed the room and there's nothing left to do besides get the food. I have no idea what Quinn said she wanted, but it doesn't matter because tacos are the only thing I can carry back.

The three workers have gone into a back room, probably to get more supplies. Now's my chance. I run out and grab two taco shells. But I accidentally knock a third one, and the rest of them fall like dominos to the floor.

"Did you hear that?" one of the women says.

"Hear what?"

The back door is pushed open. I dive down, behind a juice cart. One of the women is walking closer. And closer. I'm tickling my nose and forcing sneezes out: *Achoo! Achoo! Achoo!*

They're so weak, they'd hardly budge a fleck of dust. It seems the genie magic only works about half the time I want it to.

"Hank, you set the shells up wrong and they've fallen over again!" the woman calls.

She bends down to pick them up. I say a silent apology in my head to Hank, and run back to Quinn—run and crouch, run and crouch, run and crouch. She's been watching from the doorway this whole time, so she knows about the close call. But if she's concerned about the near miss, you can't tell. "Zack, you didn't get anything!" she complains.

"I got taco shells," I say, and I hold the crushed remains out toward her.

"No, thanks, I'll go."

A *fourth* adult is at the food stations now.

"Uh-uh, no way, it's not safe," I say. "What happened was a sign that we shouldn't be in here."

"More like a sign of how clumsy you are," she said.

Behind us the front door flies open and two kids walk in. Shaggy and Buzz Cut.

"Kids to ask!" Quinn exclaims.

I grab her arm and pull her back. "Not those kids."

"Can you believe that twerp?" Shaggy says. "I can't believe we have kitchen duty all week now. When I get my hands on Trey's little neck. . . ."

Quinn elbows me. "They know Trey!"

"We'll just make sure he's quiet next time," Shaggy says.

"Hey!" Quinn calls out.

"Stop it," I hiss. "They're Reggs–they hate Trey."

"They still might know where he lives," she says. She steps forward, toward them. "You guys know Trey? Do you know where he lives?"

"Hold up," Buzz says. "You mean to tell me you're here for the twerp?"

I step up behind Quinn and say as softly as I can, "We've got to get out of here. You've got to trust me."

"Please excuse my brother. He doesn't know how to act around people because he doesn't have any friends."

"Your brother?" Buzz asks, sputtering out a laugh.

"I know. We don't look alike. I was just telling him I thought he was switched at birth."

"Look, she's talking to herself," Shaggy says.

"Weirdo," Buzz says. "Look at her, even her hair is weird."

Quinn reaches up and pats the side of her head with hair hanging down loosely over her shoulder. "My friend just didn't finish braiding it, that's all," she says defensively. "And don't you see him?"

"Of course I see him. Helloooo, phantom brother." Buzz waves a hand toward the space on the left side of Quinn. But I'm standing on her right side.

Holy smokes! I'm invisible!

The real kind of invisible. Not the fake kind I feel most days at Pinemont Elementary.

"They can't see me," I tell Quinn, speaking softly even though I'm fairly certain they can't hear me, either. "And, Quinn, you gotta trust me when I tell you, they're not good guys. Trey's not the best guy himself, but he knows something about them–something bad."

"Trey knows something bad about them?" Quinn asks softly.

"What did you say?" Buzz asks.

"Nothing," she says quickly.

Shaggy knocks Buzz in the side. "We could get points for this." Buzz nods, and Shaggy takes a step toward the double doors. "Come with us," he tells Quinn. "We'll take you to Trey's dorm. It's in Twendel One."

Twendel One. I've heard that name before. "That's where Trey said Heddle's office is," I say. "The head of school."

Quinn takes a step back. "No, thanks. On second thought, I don't need to find Trey. I don't need your help at all."

"She's onto us," Shaggy says.

"Get her!"

13

PERKS OF INVISIBILITY

When Shaggy lunges for my sister, I stick out my leg and *SPLAT!* He's facedown on the floor. A perk of being invisible. Shaggy didn't even see it coming.

I don't even have to tell Quinn what to do next. In a split second we're both out the door and racing across the lawn. My feet are pounding the ground as hard as my heart is pounding in my chest.

Shaggy has scrambled up, and now he and Buzz are running after us. But Quinn is really dragging. "Faster, Quinn," I tell her.

"I'm going as fast as I can," she says, panting.

The Reggs are gaining on us. Up ahead, I spot the spout of a sprinkler. If only I knew how to wish it on. Maybe it would keep the Reggs off the lawn.

"Zack," Quinn says, nearly breathless. "I can't keep up."

I tuck an arm around her, sprinting faster than ever. It's like my legs are doing the work for us both. There's a roar of wind in my ears. I barely hear the *click, click* sound in the background. The sprinklers! They're on!

"My hair!" Quinn whines in my ear. "It's soaked!"

The droplets bounce off me like Ping-Pong balls. I glance behind. The Reggs are farther in the distance now, on the part on the lawn that isn't being swept with water.

"Hey, you there!" a voice rings out. "Off the grass!" Coming up behind the Reggs is a man waving a pair of garden shears in disapproval. He manages to catch up to Shaggy and Buzz.

Quinn and I have reached the sidewalk at the far end of the field. She bends over, holding her knees with her hands, trying to catch her breath. The end of her braid is drip, drip, dripping onto the cement. I know we've got to keep running, but I don't know where to.

"We just seeded the lawn," the gardener is yelling at the Reggs. "Didn't you see the sign to keep off it?"

"But that girl," Shaggy says. "She was on the grass, too, and she's getting away!"

"You worry about yourselves," I hear the gardener say. "That's the trouble with kids these days–always more concerned with what others are doing and no-accounts themselves. I'll deal with her after I deal with you."

"He's going to deal with me?" Quinn gasps.

I spin around, trying to think of where to run next, when I see the building with big black iron letters spelling it out, plain as day: PRESTON H.

"That's where Trey lives!" I say, pointing to the dorm that bears his name.

"How do you know?"

"I just do—get that key card ready." We break into a run—well, I run and drag Quinn along with me.

We're at Twendel Hall III. For a split second I think maybe I'm wrong about the dorm. Maybe Trey wouldn't want to live in a building with his name on it. But when Quinn swipes the card in the slot, it totally works.

Inside is a lobby, not as large as the one in Twendel II, but still pretty fancy. There's a dark wood floor so polished, I can practically see my face in it, and red leather wingback chairs on either side of a fireplace.

Quinn collapses into one of the chairs, while I look around. To the right is a hallway leading to dorm rooms, and a stairwell, which I guess leads to even more dorm rooms. From the outside, we could see the building was three stories tall. "Come on," I tell her. "There's no time to waste."

She trudges down the first hall with me. I'd been worried about how we'd figure out which room is Trey's, but now I see every door is decorated with a cutout of a big red balloon showing the names of the two kids who live there:

Adam Upton and Eric Ballard

Keith Washington and Derek Strausser

Gabe Pickler and Charles Martin

I don't feel bad about going into Trey's room without permission because we have his key card, and besides, technically Quinn *is* Trey now. But I feel a little strange about going into his roommate's room without permission.

I shouldn't have worried, though, because there at the end of the hallway on the third floor is the only door with just one name in the red balloon. The name that matches the name on the building: Preston H. Twendel III.

Well, to be accurate, there's another name on the balloon. It's blacked out, but I can see that the first name starts with an N and the last name ends with an X. Directly across the hall is a door with *three* names on it. The third name is squeezed in on the bottom of the balloon, and it says: Nick Marx.

My guess–this Nick Marx found out he was rooming with Trey and wasn't having it. The other kids across the way felt bad for him, and they let him move in. I feel a pang for Trey, because I know what it's like to not have friends.

But then I remind myself: I have a friend. Eli. Plus, Uncle Max, plus, my cousins. Plus, I didn't exactly think Trey was so nice when I met him, and I wouldn't want to room with him, either. *I'd* be a way better roommate. I'd keep everyone safe.

But there's still a problem. The door doesn't have a swipe thing for a key card. There's a key*pad* by the handle, and I guess to open the door you have to type in the right number combination.

Figuring that out would take hours–days even. And we don't have that kind of time.

"Now what, genie?" Quinn asks.

"I don't know," I admit.

14

Now What?

"Well?" Quinn asks.

"Shh. I'm thinking."

I sit and think about how much I want the door to open—how much I *need* it to open. It worked on the creaky door—suddenly, just because I was thinking about it, oil appeared. But nothing appears to help me with this.

"Maybe we can climb in through the window," Quinn says.

I'm about to tell her no way—I'm a genie, not Spider-Man, and do you know how many people are killed each year trying to scale the sides of buildings?–when Trey's door swings open. Out comes a woman in a maid's uniform, carrying a bucket of cleaning supplies.

"Excuse me, can you hold that?" Quinn asks.

"This is Mr. Twendel's room," the maid tells her. "No unauthorized admittance." She pulls the door shut behind her . . . but not before I whip by, quick as a wink, and squeeze in before it clicks shut.

Now that I'm on the other side, I survey things. There's one bed freshly made up with navy sheets and the puffiest comforter I've ever seen. Across the room there's another bed, completely bare. Trey doesn't have anything on the walls, but he does have a flat-screen TV and three different video game consoles.

Best of all: a computer.

There's a soft knock on the door, and then Quinn's voice: "Zack, open up. The coast is clear."

I open it up, let her in, and close it quickly behind her.

"Ooh, a bed!" Quinn cries. She flops on it, and sighs. "This is the coziest bed I've ever lain on in my life." Within seconds, her breathing deepens. I'll have to remember to tease her about her snoring habit. But right now there's the task at hand. I sit down at the computer and pull up the Skype page. Uncle Max is probably one of the last people in the world—or at least in Pinemont—to not have a computer at home. But luckily Skype lets you call actual phones. My fingers fly across the keyboard, punching in the numbers. When I finish dialing, there isn't any ringing. Just an empty kind of swirling sound, like the sound you get when you hold a shell up to your ear to hear the ocean.

Huh. Maybe I dialed wrong. I press to end the call and try again, typing slowly and pressing each of the numbers extra hard, just to make sure. But the same thing happens again. Now I know I've dialed correctly, and I hit the keyboard in frustration. What is going on?

"Huh? What was that?" Quinn asks. She sits up, blinking. "Ugh, I'm still here?" She moans.

"Yeah, and I haven't been able to get through to Uncle Max yet. I think Skype is broken."

"I'll do it," she says. She rises from the bed, as if with great effort, and pushes me aside so she can sit in Trey's–her–desk chair. I have to tell her Uncle Max's number, since she doesn't know it by heart. For a third time, the other line is just ocean sounds. She clicks to end the call and starts typing again.

"It's not gonna work," I tell her.

"I'm not calling Uncle Max," she says. "I'm calling Mom."

I stand next to her, waiting for ocean sounds again. But the line is ringing, and ringing, and . . .

"Hello?"

"Mom!" Quinn cries. "It's me! I'm in this weird place with Zack and–"

"It's not my fault!" I yell. I forget about how she probably can't see or hear me.

"Be quiet, Zack," Quinn says.

"Zack, who's Zack?" Mom says.

"Your son," Quinn tells her.

"Oh, Quinn," Mom says. "Enough nonsense."

Nonsense? Could Mom really have forgotten my entire existence?

"If you have something to tell me, don't do it over the phone," Mom continues, to Quinn. "Just walk into the other room."

"But that's what I'm trying to tell you! I'm not home! I can't walk into the other room!"

"Very funny," Mom says. "But let me go now. I'm still cleaning up from the party–unless you and Madeline want to help."

"I'm not with Madeline!"

"Honey, I can hear you giggling from the other room. I'll talk to you later."

"But, Mom–"

The line goes dead and a message pops up on-screen: Call Ended.

"How can I be there and here at the same

time?" Quinn asks.

"How can Mom not remember that she has a son?"

"Maybe she blocked it out," Quinn tells me. "It's not like I blame her."

"Yeah, well, maybe you're not even the real Quinn," I say. "Maybe you're just a copy and I don't even have to worry about getting you home."

"Zack, I'm me and I can prove it!" she says. "I know that it took you a year longer than me to be potty trained. And I know that you threw up through your nose on the first day of kindergarten. And I know you couldn't go to sleep without Ralphie, your stuffed rabbit, until you were nine. Now tell me why this is happening!"

I shrug. "Uncle Max would know."

"Well, we can't ask him, can we?" she says. "Because his phone doesn't work. Even a fake uncle should have a working phone at a time like this!"

"He's not a fake," I tell her. "He just let us believe we weren't related because it was easier, since . . ." Quinn's glaring at me. "Never mind. It doesn't matter. The point is, I bet the phone not working is something similar, an Official Genie Decision."

Quinn has taken up the keyboard again and is dialing. "Who are you calling now?" I ask.

"Not that it's any of your business, but I'm calling Bella. Maybe she can get a message to Mom."

"Mom's not going to listen to Bella," I say. "She thinks you're home safe and sound right now."

For a second Quinn's eyes look shiny. But she blinks and recovers quickly. "Fine, then. I'll tell her to get a message to Uncle Max. I don't care who she gets the message to, as long as we get out of here." She pauses. "Or at least I get out of here. You can stay here if you'd like."

"You think I want to be here?" I ask. "I want to leave as much as you do–more even."

"Doubtful."

"Do you think Bella will actually call Uncle Max without checking with Mom first?" I ask. "I mean, it does sound pretty crazy–*Hey, it's me, Quinn, and pay no attention to the fact there's another Quinn . . .*"

"Well, that's just great," Quinn says. Her voice is thick, and the tears start falling, thick ones, plop plop. My bionic genie eyes see the little splashes they make on the carpet.

"Aw, Quinn," I say, and I reach a hand out, but she bats me away. "Okay," I say. "You're mad. But I have another idea. What do you do when you NEED to talk to someone but you can't get him on the phone?"

"Am I supposed to answer?"

"You go to his house, that's what."

"You're saying we're going to walk from here to Uncle Max's?" She looks down at my feet. "Don't you think it might be too far? Plus, you don't even have shoes."

That reminds me: I should borrow a pair

of Trey's. "It's definitely too far to walk," I say. "We're in California, remember? We need to buy plane tickets. Trey–I mean you–you've got to have money for those things. Where do you keep it?"

"How would I know?" Quinn asks. But then she opens the desk drawer, and right on top is a black wallet–a really thick one. Quinn unfolds it and there's a flash of green. She pulls out a stack of twenty-dollar bills and starts counting. "Twenty. Forty. Sixty. Eighty." And on, and on. I've never actually seen so much money in one place.

"Oh my god, it's a hundred-dollar bill!" she squeals.

I've never seen a hundred-dollar bill before, either.

Quinn opens another compartment in the wallet and pulls out a credit card. I didn't know kids could have credit cards. "We could buy so much stuff with this," Quinn says. She's already punching the computer keys. Two tickets from

California to Pennsylvania. "Do you know what airport we're closest to? Do you know what airline is best?"

I shake my head.

She clicks some more keys. "We should definitely fly first class, as long as we have to fly anyway. I saw something on TV once about flying first class–you get big, comfy seats, and you can recline them back so they turn into beds. Plus, the food is really good, and you can watch all the movies you want for free." She pauses to take a breath. "Aren't you excited?"

"This isn't exciting. This is an emergency."

"Sometimes they're the same thing."

I grab the credit card from her. She lunges to grab it back, but now I'm holding it over my head and out of her reach. Seven minutes older, and about seven hundredths of an inch taller.

"Zack! Come on! Give it back! It's my credit card, not yours."

"It's not yours, either."

"It is too mine. I'm Trey. Or he's me. Whatever. Just give it back."

"Ha!" I say. "You believe me now, that I'm a genie and I turned Trey into you. Admit it!"

"Never," Quinn says.

She jumps to grab the card from me, and I push her back with my free hand. "Wait, did you hear that?"

"I don't hear anything. Don't try to distract me. Just give it back."

Knock, knock, knock.

This time we both hear it.

Quinn and I look at the door. There's no peephole. *Knock, knock, knock.* "Don't answer it," I whisper to her.

"I won't, she says.

But then there's the unmistakable sound of someone punching numbers in the keypad, and a click when the combination is right and the door unlocks. We watch as the handle turns, almost in slow motion, and then the door swings open. On the other side are two very serious-looking adults, a man and a woman. I quickly shove Trey's credit card into my pocket.

"Who are you and what are you doing here?" the man asks Quinn.

"I can't answer that for fear of incriminating myself," Quinn tells him. "I need a lawyer."

"A lawyer?" I ask. "We're just kids. We're too young to have lawyers."

"I saw it on TV," Quinn explains.

"I don't think there's a lawyer who can help with this sort of thing," I say.

"Forget what you saw on TV," the man tells her. "You're going to have to come with us."

"No. I can't go with strangers," Quinn tells him.

"Well, then I'll introduce myself. I'm Mr. Hayden. I'm Trey's history teacher." He points to the woman. "This is Ms. Lucas."

"English department," she says.

"Trey didn't show up to either of our classes

today. Dawson said he saw a girl acting strangely and inquiring about Trey's belongings when he was cleaning the chapel. Now you're trespassing in his room, and I think that's something the authorities will be interested in."

"The authorities?" I squeak out. "The police?"

"The police?" Quinn repeats. "But you can't arrest me. This is all my brother's fault."

"Come on, now," the woman says. "Don't make this more difficult than it has to be."

Ms. Lucas reaches for Quinn's hand, but Quinn jerks it away. I grab it, and Quinn grabs back, supertight. For a second I can't tell where my hand ends and hers begins. But then Mr. Hayden and Ms. Lucas each start pulling on one of Quinn's arms, and her hand seems to go right through mine. We're separate again.

"Where are you taking her?" I shout. Of course they don't answer.

"Zack!"

"Don't you worry, Quinn," I say. "I'll get

back to Pennsylvania on my own. And when I get there, I'll make sure Uncle Max gets you back to real life."

"You better hurry, Zack," Quinn says as she's hustled out the door. The door closes behind the three of them, leaving me alone to fix everything.

15

The Mouth of the Roof

"Weren't you scared?" I imagine Drew Listerman asking me, because of course he'll want to interview me about all this for the Channel 7 news: *A Day in the Life of a Ten-Year-Old Genie.* I see myself shaking my head as the camera pans in super close.

"There was no time to be scared, Drew," I tell him in my most serious voice. "There was too much work to do."

But in real life, I am terrified. I'm alone again, and I have no idea where Mr. Hayden and Ms. Lucas have taken my sister. No one can see or hear me. I can't get in touch with Uncle Max, and I don't know where the closest airport is, or the phone number of a cab company to get me there.

And if I figured out where I was going, and I found a cab company to take me there, I couldn't make a phone call to a cab company because the dispatcher wouldn't be able to hear my voice. And let's say I made a reservation online. Even then, when the driver came to pick me up, he wouldn't be able to see me get into his car, so he certainly wouldn't take me where I was going. He'd just turn around and go back to the cab company and wait for instructions to take someone else somewhere else.

I suppose I could just get into a random cab and hope it eventually picked up another passenger who had to go to the airport. But that could take all day. That could take all week!

New idea: I'll take the bus. Buses have to make all their stops, whether they can see and hear their passengers or not.

I sit down in front of Trey's computer and type "Millings Academy" into Google. Apparently it's located in Grovestand, California. A little more googling, and I find out the closest airport is Orange County International, and that there's a flight to Pennsylvania leaving in three hours. Plenty of time.

I don't click the button to buy a ticket, because I don't need a ticket. No one will see me to stop me from getting on the plane anyway. But I decide to keep Trey's credit card in case I need it later.

"And that's how it's done, Drew," I say out loud.

Now to Trey's closet, because I need shoes and he's got a rack full of them. Multiple pairs of sneakers and flip-flops, each as clean as if they had just come out of the box. Plus, he has a row of half a dozen pairs of loafers—the kind my dad used to wear to work. Work shoes, Dad called them. He had a pair in black and a pair in brown, and he'd switch them up depending on the color of suit he was wearing. On weekends he wore sandals in the summer and sneakers in the winter.

I haven't seen Dad's shoes in a long time and I wonder what happened to all of them.

I'm not wearing a suit, or even khakis like Trey and the Reggs, but I take a pair of work shoes anyway. They are a little big on me, and I know I shouldn't wear shoes that are too big. Do you know how many people trip and fall when their shoes are too big? And do you know if you have a bad enough fall, you could die?

If something happened to me, I'd never be able to rescue Quinn.

I decide to double up on socks, but just as I'm opening the top dresser drawer, there's another knock on the door. I freeze in place. "No one's answering," I hear a voice say from out in the hall. A voice I know: Buzz Cut's voice.

"Let's break it," another voice answers. Shaggy this time. "Gimme a screwdriver."

"I don't have a screwdriver," Buzz says. "Credit cards work, though. I've seen them used on TV."

"Do you have one of those?"

I finger the credit card in my pocket. *Ha ha ha, Reggs.*

"Nope. But I have a library card."

"You have a library card?" Shaggy asks, incredulous.

"Ms. Corson made us sign up on the first day of school. I put it in my bag and forgot about it. May as well be put to good use."

"The best use."

There's no time to barricade the door with chairs or the dresser, so I'm just waiting for them on the other side. But when they come in and I try to shove them away, my hands go through them. I wind up facedown on the floor.

Note to self: Genie hands still get rug burns.

"Oh, man, it looks like a regular dorm room," Shaggy is saying as I rub my sore palms and get back up on my feet.

"What'd you expect?" Buzz asks him.

"I don't know . . . maybe a king-size bed and a private bathroom and a terrace. Definitely a terrace."

"If he had a terrace, we'd be able to see it from outside the building. He still has good stuff, though–look at his computer. It's way nicer than yours."

"Should I take it?" Shaggy asks.

"No, moron, we can't take it if we want to frame him."

"Oh, right," Shaggy says.

Buzz moves toward the desk chair. "Do you have the flash drive? I'll stick it in the side port and load the papers on. When we tell Heddle, Trey won't be able to deny it. The evidence will be right there. And then *who's* the cheater?"

"Brilliant," Shaggy says. He pulls the flash drive from his pocket and hands it to Buzz.

"Huh, well, look at this." Shaggy stands and

looks over Buzz's shoulder at the monitor. "Looks like our friend was planning a little trip."

"I wonder what's in Pennsylvania."

"Maybe a twerp convention."

Shaggy and Buzz break into laughter, like it's the funniest thing they've ever heard. I don't have time for this. I put my hand on the door handle, but just before I turn it, something occurs to me: They can't see me, but they can see the website I pulled up on the computer.

The inspiration hits me like a flash of lightning: Maybe I can spook them into telling me where the bottle is.

I run over to the desk and reach a hand between them to grab the mouse. I click to pull up a blank page.

"Why's the screen changing?" Buzz asks.

Then I type. I'm not so fast at typing, but the guys are staring at the screen like it's the most interesting thing in the world: I have a question.

"Dude, the computer has a question,"

Shaggy says.

"Do you think it's a ghost?"

"No, moron. It's a computer game." He reaches to punch Buzz in the shoulder, and his hand passes through my arm as he does it. Why can I touch some things same as always, like door handles and computers, but then people's hands go right through me?

But I can't let this stuff distract me right now. I keep typing. Where's the bottle?

"The bottle?" Buzz says. "What kind of game asks about a bottle?"

No time for games, I type. Where is Trey's bottle?

"Whoa," Buzz says. "I have a question for you."

I asked you first.

"This computer has an attitude problem," Shaggy says. "Kind of like its owner." He hits at the keys to erase my words.

I wouldn't do that if I were you.

Shaggy is about to press the delete key again, but Buzz stops him. "I don't like this," he says quietly.

I type three more words: Tell me, Jake.

Shaggy falls over backward. Buzz is still staring at the screen, mouth hanging open, so I add: You look surprised, Ollie.

At this point, Shaggy has scrambled up from the floor. He and Ollie race out of the room as if they're afraid the computer will chase them. I bet they spend the rest of the day trying to convince their friends that what they saw really happened and that they're not crazy. All because of my observational skills. Now that's *noggining*.

Noggining. Verb. The act of using your noggin, which is what Dad called my head.

Oh, Dad. I wish you back. I wish you were here right now. It's the only wish I need.

But of course Dad is *not* here. I grab a pair of flip-flops from Trey's closet, the closest kind of shoe to a one-size-fits-all, and then turn back to the computer and pull up a map of Grovestand, California, on Google. I find the closest bus stop to the school–I have to walk to Hollyhock Drive, make a left on Poppy Lane, and walk another block down, then I'll be there. I'm a little nervous because I'll have to cross two streets to get there. Not that I haven't crossed streets by myself before. Because I have. Of course I have–I even did it in New York City the time I got separated from Uncle Max.

But in New York City, the streets are really crowded. I thought that made it more dangerous. But now that I think about it, it's a little bit safer, too. Even when you're alone, you're not really alone.

I doubt there will be so many people on the streets in this city. And even if there are, no one can see me! What if I trip and fall in the middle of the crosswalk and a car comes speeding through and runs me over because I'm invisible to the driver?

I've never before felt so completely all on my own. I gather up all the bravery I have and walk out the door. I head to Hollyhock Drive and down a block. Then I have to cross the first street. I look both ways about five times, because you can never be too careful, step off the curb, and–*WHAM!*

It wasn't a car, but I was sure hit by something, and now colors are swirling all around me, so fast, like someone put a rainbow in a blender. It feels like something is pulling me back and back and back.

Could it be that I'm being pulled home?

Suddenly there's a loud *SNAP!*, like a giant rubber band was stretched and let go. The wind is rushing in my ears as I fly forward. I think I can make out something in the distance. The roof of a building. I'm headed straight toward it! And there's no sign of slowing down.

I don't want to die I don't want to die I don't want to die.

I can't bear to look, so I squeeze my eyes shut tight. But then I open just one eye a crack, and the weirdest, coolest thing is happening–the roof of the building is opening up like a giant mouth. I sail right through and land on my feet with a thud.

"Zack!" Quinn shouts.

16

THERE SHE GOES AGAIN

"There she goes again."

It's Ms. Lucas talking. She's here in this large, square room. There are floor-to-ceiling bookshelves against every wall, except the back wall, which is all windows. A couple of oversized red leather chairs are set in front of a huge dark-brown wood desk. Ms. Lucas is in one of the chairs, and Mr. Hayden is in the other. Quinn is standing between them. And there's another man, sitting behind the desk. He's got a thick rug of hair on his head, and his face is as round as a bowling ball. The nameplate in front of him says:

E. M. HEDDLE, HEAD OF SCHOOL.

"There she goes what again, Helen?" Mr. Heddle asks.

"Zack," Ms. Lucas explains. For a split second, she turns her head in the direction Quinn is facing, but instead of looking at me, it's like she's looking through me. A chill shoots down my spine.

Ms. Lucas faces Heddle again and goes on, "She keeps calling out to someone–"

"My brother!" Quinn interrupts.

"Who isn't here," Ms. Lucas finishes.

"He's here, I swear," Quinn says.

Ms. Lucas folds her arms across her chest. "I advise you to stop lying, miss."

"I'm not lying!" Quinn says. She drops her voice to a pleading tone. "I know you don't believe me–I didn't believe Zack, either. But I swear on my life that he's in this room. I don't know why we're here, or how he made himself invisible. But it's all true."

Ms. Lucas shakes her head, exasperated.

The phone rings on Mr. Heddle's desk, and he pushes a button to silence it. Then Mr. Hayden pipes up. "You know, Helen, I actually believe she's telling the truth," he says. "At least I believe that *she* thinks she is."

I recognize the look Mr. Hayden gives Quinn, because it's a look that Quinn has given me about a billion times. A look that says: *You are such a nut job.*

I always thought it would feel good to see Quinn get a taste of her own medicine. But it doesn't. Not even a little bit.

"I'm so tired," my sister says quietly. "I just want to go home. I wish I could go home."

I wiggle my toes in Trey's flip-flops. They feel like regular toes.

"I'm sorry," Mr. Heddle tells her. "But wishing isn't going to make it so."

I may be a genie, but I'm afraid he's right about that.

"It's my opinion that we should get this young girl some much-needed medical help," Mr. Hayden goes on. "Should I call in Nurse Corridan? Or better yet, perhaps I should take her straight to the emergency room."

"An emergency room?" Quinn asks. "At a hospital?"

"They could give you the help you need," Mr. Hayden tells her.

Quinn turns to me and shakes her head. Mr. Hayden probably thinks she's talking to him, but she's talking to me: "I won't go to an emergency room," she says.

I know why she won't. An emergency room is where they brought Dad.

"My car is just out back," Mr. Hayden says. "Unless you think we should call an ambulance."

"That won't be necessary," Mr. Heddle says.

"Thank you," Quinn says. There is relief in her voice, but it only lasts about two seconds. "But wait, do you mean calling an ambulance isn't necessary, or going to the hospital at all?"

"Helen, Colin," Mr. Heddle says to the teachers. "You can go back to your classrooms now. I can take it from here."

Mr. Hayden and Ms. Lucas rise from their seats. Mr. Heddle waits until the door closes behind them, and then he holds a hand out. "I know you're tired. You should take a seat." Quinn eyes the oversized red chairs but doesn't move toward them. "Go on," Mr. Heddle tells her. "Make yourself at home."

My sister moves slowly to the chair on the left and sits down on the edge of it. I take the one on the right–like Quinn, I'm right at the edge. It's hard to sit back and make yourself at home when you have no idea what will happen next or if you'll ever make it back to your real home again.

"Thanks," Quinn says.

"Can I get you anything?" Mr. Heddle goes on. "Water? A bag of chips?"

"I'm okay," Quinn tells him.

"Oh, come on," Mr. Heddle says. "You look like you could use a little pick-me-up. How about both?"

"Okay," Quinn says, nodding. "I actually am pretty hungry–and thirsty, too. I wanted to get something at Food Hall. But Zack . . ." Her voice trails off, knowing Mr. Heddle probably won't believe what she says anyway. He opens a desk drawer and pulls out a bottle of spring water and a bag of barbecue chips–my favorite–and places them in front of Quinn. My stomach grumbles. "Gross, Zack," Quinn whispers out the side of her mouth.

"It's been a while since I've eaten, too," I remind her.

"And whose fault is that?"

"Go easy on your brother," Mr. Heddle says. "It looks like he's had a long day, too."

Looks like? He can *see* me?

He's staring at me–at me, not through me.

"You can see Zack?" Quinn squeaks out.

"I sure can," he says.

"How?" I ask.

E. M. Heddle cracks a smile. He pulls another bag of chips out from a drawer and tosses them my way. Then he folds his hands together and leans forward over the desk. I hesitate opening the bag because, well, it just seems weird that he can see me. But I guess it's even weirder that no one else can. "Sit back," he says. "Relax. Eat."

I can't think of anything else to do, so I rip open the bag and pop a chip into my mouth. "How can you see me and no one else can?"

"Don't talk with your mouth full," Quinn tells me, as if *that's* what I should be worried about right now. She turns to Mr. Heddle. "Please believe me when I say I have no idea what happened to that kid—to Trey. Zack keeps telling me he's a genie and Trey wished to turn into me, or something like that."

"I do believe you," Mr. Heddle says. "Do you believe him?"

"I don't know!" Quinn says. "I didn't think so. But I don't know what the real explanation could be. So many things are happening that I can't explain. Like, those teachers didn't believe me that Zack was invisible, and I knew he was right there." She puts her bottle of water down, hard, and a bit sloshes out onto the desk. "Sorry," she says.

"That's all right," Mr. Heddle tells her.

"It's just hard to know what to believe," Quinn says softly, shaking her head. "I wish someone would be straight with me about what I'm doing here."

"I wish–" I start.

"Ah, ah, ah," Mr. Heddle says, shaking a finger at me. "You don't want to waste your wish–trust me."

Just like Uncle Max did, he licks a finger and holds it in the air. "Mr. Heddle?" Quinn asks.

"I'm not who you think I am," he says.

"Who are you?" I ask.

"The question isn't who I am," he says. "It's who *you* are."

"Who *I* am?"

"You're a seventh-family genie," he says.

"How do you know that?" I ask.

"Because I'm a genie, too," he says.

"That's why you can see me!"

"Indeed it is. Mortals can only hear, see, and feel what they expect. But we genies know to expect the unexpected, and we see everything."

"So you can help us!" I say. "We're trying to get home–or at least get in touch with my uncle Max."

"You can help yourself," he says.

"How?"

"We'll get to that. We'll get to everything, little sparkie."

"Sparkie?" I repeat.

"That's what new young genies, such as yourself, are called–your powers come out in fits and sparks. You haven't figured out how to harness your power and use it at will."

"I'll say," I tell him. "Sometimes things happen because I want them to, and sometimes nothing happens at all. And I don't know what I'm doing differently."

"That's perfectly normal," he tells me. "But give yourself some credit, too. After all, your sister is here because you successfully used your powers to grant a wish. That young man, Trey, wished to be someone else, did he not?"

"He did," I say.

Mr. Heddle–or Mr. *not* Heddle–nods. "And that turned out to be Quinn."

"But . . . But . . ." Quinn sputters. "But when we tried to call my mom, she said I was *there* at home."

"That was a brilliant play on your brother's part–he did a Rutherford split. Part of you is here, and part of you is there. Neither part realizes she is simply a piece of a whole."

He snaps his fingers, and a white shade falls

down over the window on the far wall. The room is suddenly darker, and a movie begins to play with the shade as a screen.

No, wait. It's not a movie. It's Quinn! Quinn and Madeline! They are sitting on the bed in Quinn's room. Unlike the Quinn here at MA with me, the Quinn on the screen has both sides of her hair in braids. She and Madeline are bent over their toenails, painting them a rainbow of colors. I watch Mom enter the room and say something about putting towels down and not spilling polish on the comforter.

"That's me," Quinn says. Her voice is barely a whisper.

"That's the *other* half of you," Mr. Heddle says. He turns to me. "Well done, young man."

"Uh. Thanks," I say.

"But wait," Quinn says. "Is it dangerous that I've been split in two?"

Mr. Heddle shrugs. "Whole people are always stronger than the individual parts," he says.

"Zack, how could you do that to me?" I turn to her to apologize, but my sister is yawning. She leans back against the red leather chair. "It's too much," she says. "I think I need to close my eyes for a bit."

I feel a bit light-headed, too. Maybe I made a sparkie mistake and accidentally did a Rutherford split on myself. Because the room seems to be spinning.

Oh, wait. The room is actually spinning! The walls are moving around us. I haven't moved a muscle, and yet I feel myself rising up, up, up. I reach down to grab the chair beneath me, but it's hard to get a good grip when things are going in circles. I manage to pull at the piping on the back of the chair with the tips of my fingers. But then I continue to rise and I can't even do that anymore. Below me, my sleeping sister is getting farther and farther away.

Mr. Heddle shoots up next to me. The fake Mr. Heddle. I'm still thinking of him as

E. M. Heddle in my head because I don't know his real name, whoever he is. Around us, the sky is dark except for the glow of stars like lights on a Christmas tree. I swing my legs around, trying to figure out if I can make myself move back down. Trey's flip-flops fall off, one after the other, and I can hear them whistling to the ground.

"Oh no!" I cry. "Watch out, Quinn!"

But she's too far away—and fast asleep—to hear me.

"You sound concerned," Mr. Heddle says.

"Well, yeah, of course," I say. "Do you know how many people are killed each year by things that fly out of windows, or off roofs of buildings? A shoe falling from this height—that's gotta be deadly."

"I suppose it would be," Mr. Heddle says calmly, evenly.

"Plus, we're just floating in space. I get maybe that's a genie thing, but I still prefer solid ground."

"If that's what you prefer," Mr. Heddle says. And with a snap of his fingers, a floor materializes under my swinging feet.

"Where are we now?" I say as my feet test the ground.

Mr. Heddle keeps snapping. A chair knocks me gently from behind, and I fall into it. Beside me a floor lamp appears, and a little coffee table. "Put your feet up," he says. "This is the thirteenth parallel, where we aim to make our guests comfortable so they'll want to stay."

"And Quinn?"

"Don't you worry about Quinn," he says. "Let's talk about your heart's desires. You wanted a dog, right? A dog just for you and no one else? Do you still want one?"

"Sure, I guess. But now doesn't seem the time . . ."

"Nonsense! I won't even make you wish for it. This one will be a freebie."

I spot something in the distance. At first it's

just a dot, like the sparkle of a star. But it's moving closer and closer, running toward me, seemingly through the air. Before I can blink, the world's cutest golden Labrador puppy has jumped up next to me. It settles its head in my lap. Could this really be happening? I lower a hand to the dog's back. It certainly feels like a real dog.

"Check out the tag," Mr. Heddle says.

I feel around the dog's neck for the collar and look at the name tag: I BELONG TO ZACK COOLEY, it reads.

"You should name it. A dog needs a name. Speaking of which, I haven't properly introduced myself, have I?"

"No," I say. My voice is barely a whisper.

"I am Linx. I am the head of the thirteenth family."

17

History Lesson

"Linx," I repeat.

Before my eyes, the man who was E. M. Heddle starts to transform. He grows taller and broader. Thick hairs sprout from the top of his head and flow back in waves like water. The whites of his eyes go whiter, so white they practically glow. And his pupils turn red—which is incidentally the same color that his skin has become.

I pull the puppy closer, onto my lap, and bury my face in its silky tan fur.

"Don't be scared," Linx tells me. His voice

has changed, too. It sounds as deep as the ocean. "I'm not going to hurt you. You believe me, right?"

I look up. There in front of me, Linx looks more like a monster than a man. But I find myself nodding anyway, almost involuntarily, like I'm in a trance.

"That's good," he says. He stretches his arms out, as wide as a pterodactyl's wingspan. "Whoa, it feels good to be out of Heddle's body. It was getting a little cramped in there. Those of us in the thirteenth have always been a bit bigger than average."

Understatement of the year. Next to Linx, the guy cleaning up the chapel was practically the size of a toddler. "Did you say the *thirteenth* family?" I ask.

"Indeed," Linx says. "But I bet your uncle Max told you there were twelve genie families."

"You know Uncle Max?"

"Max and I go way back," Linx says. "Way back to the womb. So I know he has a tendency to lie when he needs to. Tell me this, Zack, has Max ever lied to you before?"

"No," I say. But as soon as the word is out of my mouth, I remember—he lied about how we were related, and he lied about being a genie, and he lied about my being one, too.

"Ah, Zack. Really?"

"Uncle Max loves us a lot. After my dad died, he . . ." I let my voice trail off. "Anyway, like I was saying before, my sister and I just want to go home."

"Here, Zack, catch." Linx throws me a doggie treat. The puppy laps it from my palm, licking each of my fingers like they're lollipops. It's hard to tell just what is real. But this dog certainly feels real. "You still haven't named him. It's not right for a dog to go nameless."

I shake my head. "I can't think of any."

"Titan? Flash? Goliath? Hercules?" Linx suggests, and I shrug. "Well, you think on it. In the meantime, I have a story to tell you. Years ago, years and years ago–before you were even a figment of your parents' imaginations, before your parents were figments of your grandparents' imaginations, and centuries before that–the thirteenth genie family was the most powerful genie family in all the world, and I was the most powerful genie."

Linx pauses for a moment and smiles, like he's remembering fondly.

"Mortals would find my bottle and rub it," he goes on. "But as you know, merely rubbing a genie bottle is not enough to summon a genie."

"I didn't know that," I tell him.

"Mmm, it seems that uncle of yours is a little behind in your education. Allow me to enlighten you–as a rule, only a man in distress can get a genie to emerge."

"Trey isn't a man," I say. "He is a boy–a kid, like me."

"My dear Zack," Linx says. "Trey was most certainly not 'like you.' But I see your point–a man, or a woman, or a *child* must be in distress, and rub the bottle at that very moment. And when that happens, the magic kicks in."

"Trey said he rubbed the bottle before," I remember, out loud. "But today was when Shaggy and Buzz–these other kids–were attacking him in the chapel. So that's gotta be what made the difference. He was in distress."

"Precisely. You're catching on fast. And then you popped out of the bottle and Trey made his wish and you–"

"And I messed it all up."

"Nonsense! You *interpreted* his wish, that's all. Back when I was granting wishes, I prided myself on my creativity when it came to wish interpretation. For example, there was a man who'd never had as much money as those around him. He made a wish to be richer than all of his neighbors, and I banished him to Antarctica, where he was certainly the richest–he didn't have any neighbors! Unless you count the penguins and the whale seals.

Another time a woman with a rather unfortunate face wished that people would think she was beautiful. I turned her into a rose, and people certainly exclaimed over her beauty after that."

"That's not what they meant," I say.

"Are you sure about that? Were you in their heads?"

"No, but anyone could tell," I say. "Like I could tell Trey didn't really want me to turn him into Quinn—and Quinn sure didn't want me to split her into two and drag her here."

"You know, Zack, you remind me of myself, when I was young. I think you may take after me. You worry about other people, and not having control. I have so much to teach you. And lesson number one is that control is what being a genie is all about. You can make things happen, simply by force of will."

I'm shaking my head. Because I don't know how to make anything happen.

"I worked to empower the genie community,"

Linx goes on. "Not just the thirteenth family, but all genies. Genies like you. That's all I was trying to do until someone stopped me. He would've killed me, if he'd had the chance."

I suck in my breath. Words echo in my ears: *I've only come close to killing someone once.*

"You know who I'm talking about, don't you?" Linx asks.

"Uncle Max," I whisper.

"Yes. He turned everyone against me. And then, with the force of the other families behind him, he banished me and my entire family here, to the thirteenth parallel, for a few dozen centuries."

"Centuries?"

"You have no idea how hard it's been, being up here," Linx says. "We have a window down to the world, but we can't access it."

"How did you escape?"

"It was you."

"Me?"

"You see how powerful you are. You broke

a force field that had the strength of twelve genie families, by providing the portal for me to break through."

"Portal? My bottle? You came through my bottle?"

Linx reaches behind him and produces my scuffed-up green bottle. The bottle I'd been bummed out to get for a birthday present. Now I'm so happy to see it! I worried I'd never see it again! I reach for it, but Linx holds it back, too far for my fingers to grasp. "I wasn't supposed to lose sight of it," I explain. "Uncle Max said bad things would happen."

"It allowed me to come back. Nothing bad has happened, has it? You have a puppy. Would you like another?" Before I can answer, a chocolate-brown Lab trots across the floor. "Two dogs in one day. That's not so bad for one birthday boy, now is it?"

"What about Quinn?" I ask. "We're twins, you know. It's her birthday, too. And I think all she wants is to go back home."

"Are you really worried about what Quinn wants right now?" Linx asks. He's got the bottle hovering just above his flattened palm. It's spinning slowly, around and around, and the way the light from the stars is hitting it, it seems to be changing colors. "When has she ever been worried about you?"

Somewhere, deep in the background, I think I can hear a phone ringing. But I'm not sure. I can't quite make the sound out. It's like when you wake up and you sort of remember your dream, but not enough to actually know what it was about.

"Watch this, Zack." Linx snaps his fingers, and the bottle shines bright green, like an emerald. Brighter and brighter. There are claps of thunder and then lightning flashes striking the bottle. Linx cackles, and I squeeze my eyes shut. But even with them closed I can still see the brightness of the bottle hovering above his hand.

And then it starts to dim. I open one eye just a slit, and the bottle is glowing like a night-light.

"Power," Linx says. "It means I can take all the light from all the stars in the world and put it here in this bottle. And with a wink of my eye, I can disperse it again, throughout the sky. I can make the sky explode within a storm, and just as quickly I can make the storm dissipate."

"Holy smokes," I whisper.

"Without power, I'm just as helpless as young Trey, being beat up by the bullies. Your uncle was my bully, Zack. He took away my power. But you've given it back to me. And in return, I'm willing to grant your dearest wish."

18

My Dearest Wish

"I know my dearest wish," I tell Linx.

"I knew you would, Zack. I knew you would."

"But do I really get to make it? Uncle Max said I couldn't make wishes for myself. He said the genie bite means I'm supposed to do that for others." I lift my right leg and wiggle my big toe. Both of the dogs turn their heads to look at the squiggle and dot, and their ears perk up like maybe it's a bone or a ball for them to play with. "He said *that* was my destiny."

"Don't you worry about what Max said," Linx tells me. "We just determined that he isn't the most trustworthy genie, didn't we? Didn't he lie to you–about many things, over the course of many years?"

My gut twists because I have to nod. Uncle Max *did* lie to me. "He had his reasons," I say quietly.

Without thinking about it, I reach a hand toward my foot, but Linx's voice is loud and stops me mid-reach: "Don't touch that! Don't even think about it! You have a wish to make!"

He's right. I do have a wish, and I can feel the words of my wish building inside me, like they are physical objects. They feel heavy and important.

"I wish," I begin. My toe tingles. I fold my leg up and I squeeze my toe as I keep going, "that my dad–"

"GET YOUR HAND OFF YOUR FOOT!" Linx roars at me, sending a gale-force wind from his mouth that practically blows my hair off my head. The dogs both jump off the chair and hide behind it, whimpering. My heart is *boom-boom*ing in my chest. Partly from the weight of what I was about to say, but mostly because Linx has just yelled louder than I've ever heard anyone yell in my life. His words are still echoing in my ears.

"I'm . . . I'm sorry," I stutter. "I didn't know–" But then I cut myself off. Because something is emerging from the green bottle hovering above Linx's palm. Or I should say some*one*.

"Uncle Max!" I cry.

It's him!

Or at least it's his head, getting larger and larger at the top of the bottle, like a balloon that's being blown up. When it gets to its regular size, he says, "Hello, Zachary. It seems you've summoned me in the nick of time."

"I summoned you? How?"

"You squeezed your toe," Uncle Max said.

"My toe? This whole time, *that's* how I could've reached you?"

"You needed to have your bottle close by,

too," Uncle Max says. "But it is indeed."

"Holy smokes," I say. "I can see through your head. I mean, when you talk–I can see straight through your mouth to the sky behind you. It's transparent, or translucent, or something."

"It's a hologram," Uncle Max explains. "I'm here, but I'm not entirely here."

"And he's no concern of yours," Linx says. "Just squeeze your toe again and send him packing. You've got an important wish to make."

"I know I do," I say. "It's just I've been trying to reach him for so long." I look back at the Max-head. "First I called, but it didn't even ring. It just sounded like . . . like emptiness. I'm sure that's another safety measure."

The hologram head nods. "Genie Board Decision one thousand three."

"But it's actually not safe at all," I go on. "I didn't know what I was doing, and there was no one else to call because they couldn't see or hear me! Mom didn't even remember that I existed! I thought I'd fly home to you. I was going to take a bus to the airport to get on a plane to come home. But when I got off the MA campus, I was shot back here like a rubber band."

"Until the mission is complete, you can't travel more than a quarter mile from your genie assignment," Uncle Max says. "But listen to me, Zack. Right now I need to talk to you about your wish."

"No, Zack," Linx says. "You don't need to consult anyone about your wish. You just have to make it. Tell me—what is the one thing that's been missing from your life? What is it that you wish?"

"Don't say it out loud," Uncle Max says.

"Don't. Listen. To. Him," Linx says. The words come out in sharp punches, like a fist pounding in anger. But when I gasp, he softens his voice. "It won't hurt to say what you've been thinking," he says, almost sweetly. "Just say the words. *I wish . . .*"

"You only get one wish," Uncle Max says. "You've got to wish him away. There are consequences to every action. You can't even begin to understand the consequences if you don't send Linx away."

"But what about the consequence of getting Dad back?" I ask. "Isn't that the one that matters the most?"

"That's right, Zack," Linx says. "That's all that matters."

"Your dad is gone, Zack," Uncle Max says. "It's a terrible thing, but you have to move forward. Even in the genie world, that's what you have to do."

"He's lying again, Zack. You don't have to do anything you don't want to. And you want your dad—more than anything."

"Linx is using what he knows about you," Uncle Max says. "Remember when I broke the genie news to you this afternoon—I told you how much you can learn about a person by what his wishes are, and that needs to be handled with care."

"Of course I know things about you," Linx breaks in. "I used to be the most powerful genie in the world. Why else do you think my b–I mean *your uncle* wanted to banish me? He was jealous. He was so jealous, he couldn't even see straight. But now that you've brought me back, I have the power to make your dearest wish come true. Maybe your uncle can't change the past, but I can. You can trust me, Zack. *I've* never lied to you."

"You only get one wish," Uncle Max says. "You must wish him gone. It's the only way to set things right."

"You're in control, Zack. You don't have to do anything he says. Don't wish me gone. Wish *him* back."

My head keeps turning back and forth between Uncle Max and Linx, like I'm watching a tennis match.

"You can have him back, Zack. It just takes

one wish. It's yours to make. Nothing else will matter."

"No," Uncle Max says. "There are *always* other things that matter. Don't you want to rescue Quinn? You can't do it if you give your one wish to the past."

"Don't worry about what your uncle says," Linx says. "And don't worry about your sister. Think of yourself. Think of Zacktastic."

Zacktastic! Dad's name for me!

"You don't need any of the rest of them."

The whole time they've been arguing, my heart has been beating to the words: *I wish I could have my dad back.* The words have been at the tip of my tongue, and my eyes are brimming with tears. But at that moment, when Linx says that– *you don't need anyone else*–something snaps in me, like the breaking of a spell.

Dad would've wanted me to worry about Quinn. Because she was one of the most important people in his life. He would've done anything to protect her. And that's what he would've wanted me to do right now.

I miss Dad as much as ever, and my heart is pounding with all the love I ever had for him, and all the sadness I ever felt since he's been gone.

But there's only one thing to do.

19

ACCEPTANCE

Every feeling I've ever had is bubbling up inside me, like my body is a pot set on the stove to boil. "I wish Linx was gone," I say.

There's a sound, like a snap. This time I think I know what it means. "Stand back, Zack," Uncle Max tells me.

Uncle Max is a whole person now, outside the bottle. His hair is slicked back in waves, and he licks his index finger and whisks it through the air. A beam of light hits Linx in the center of his forehead. His skin glows at the spot, and then it travels through his body. Pretty soon he's all lit

up, from the inside out. The light from inside him
casts a glow over everything, including me. I hold
up a hand to shield my eyes from Linx's red light.

Linx snarls and moans and twists, like a wild
animal. Around and around and around Uncle
Max's finger goes, and when he points again, Linx
flashes in different colors—purple, blue, sparkling
glitter. All the while he is shrinking smaller and

smaller, until he's gone completely. Some sparkles remain, like fairy dust. I watch them until they, too, disappear.

"Did you kill him?" I ask.

Uncle Max shakes his head. "I couldn't even if I tried," he says. "Genie Board Decision number nine."

"So where is he?"

"In the thirteenth parallel," Uncle Max says.

"The thirteenth parallel," I repeat. "Isn't that where we–?"

Ruff!

I turn in time to see both of the dogs disappear, first the light one, then the dark one. *Poof! Poof!* And then the floor is gone, too. Uncle Max and I hover for a few seconds, and then we begin to drop. It's a floating kind of falling, down and down and down, until my feet gently find the ground. Real ground, in Mr. Heddle's office. I whiplash my head around, looking for Quinn, but she's nowhere in sight.

"Don't worry about your sister," Uncle Max says. "Her two halves are whole again, and back at home."

"What about Mom?"

"What about her?"

"Does she remember I exist?"

"When you are away on genie business, she doesn't. No one does. But when you return, it'll be like you never left them. Keeps things seamless on our end."

I nod. "And what about him?" I ask. E. M. Heddle, the real one, is slumped down at his desk.

"He's sleeping it off," Uncle Max tells me. "It's exhausting when someone borrows your body. When he wakes up, this whole experience will seem like a dream, and the memory of it will fade in a matter of seconds." Uncle Max lifts his left hand to push back the lock of floppy white hair that has fallen in front of his face. In his right hand is the bottle–my bottle–and he hands it over. "I'm sorry you had to learn all of this the hard way, but I trust you'll take better care of that from now on."

"I will," I say. "I promise. I won't ever let it out of my sight. I won't close my eyes and go to sleep. I won't even go to the bathroom."

"I'm glad you're willing to be so dedicated," Uncle Max says. "But there are a lot of ways to keep your eyes on the bottle. You'll learn all about it in school."

"They teach this stuff in school?" I ask incredulously. I've been in school for practically my whole life, and I can't think of anything close to genie stuff I've ever learned. "Are there special classes? How many other genies are there at Pinemont Elementary?"

"This is a different school," Uncle Max says. "School for Genies."

"School for Genies," I say. I can't believe it. I picture the words carved into a big wooden sign like Millings Academy: SCHOOL FOR GENIES. Everyone would wear matching shirts with SFG stitched into the pockets.

SFG!

Like on my bottle!

"And to your question on other genies," Uncle Max says. "You're the only one at Pinemont, so you won't know anyone else when you get to SFG, but you'll make new friends."

"I don't actually have too many old ones."

"I think you'll find you have a lot in common with your SFG classmates."

"Will they all be sparkies, like me?"

"How do you know about sparkies?"

"Linx told me," I say. "He said that's why sometimes my magic worked, but most of the time it didn't."

Uncle Max nods. "One of the few things Linx said that you can believe," he said. "You'll get the hang of it. SFG classes will be on Tuesdays and Thursdays."

"But what about our Tuesday and Thursday adventures?"

"Why do you think we had those adventures, Zack?"

"To have fun? To make up for the fact that Dad was gone?"

"If they were fun and gave you any comfort, then that's certainly a bonus," Uncle Max says. "But I was also trying to prepare you for all of this." He points a finger at the bottle, and I feel it buzz between my hands. "I wanted to show you that there's a time to be scared, but there's also a time to be brave, and sometimes those happen at the exact same time. I wanted you to realize you can do brave things, entirely on your own, when you are called upon to do so."

"That's why you left me at the Empire State Building last year," I say.

Uncle Max nods. "And you made it back to the hotel," he says. "You're supposed to start school next semester, but I think we can arrange for an early start. A lot of exciting adventures await you. And a lot of responsibilities, too. I think you learned that."

I nod. "I'm sorry I lost the bottle."

"No permanent damage done," Uncle Max says. "But we may not be so lucky next time, so there can't be a next time. Linx has been waiting for this moment."

"For a genie to leave a bottle unattended?"

"For *you* to leave the bottle unattended," Uncle Max says. "It has to be you, for him to come back. Even though it was a Genie Board decision, I'm the one who officially banished him. The only way for him to return is through the bottle of one of my descendants."

"Holy smokes," I say so softly that my words come out like a breath. "What would've happened if I hadn't called you when I did?"

"I don't know," Uncle Max says, shaking his head. "That's what's so dangerous about Linx. He's like a storm, and storms are unpredictable."

I shudder, thinking about lightning and how you never know where it will strike. "So it's me–

just me–standing between him coming back or not."

My uncle nods. "I'm sorry, Zack," he says. "But it seems this was part of your destiny."

There's that word again: *destiny.* "If things are destined," I say, "then why does it matter what we do at all? Aren't they going to happen anyway?"

"The universe sets things in motion," Uncle Max says. "But we're the ones who decide what to do with them."

"Like granting wishes."

"Yes, exactly. In that way, we're all unpredictable. We're all potential storms, I suppose."

"But at least when I granted Trey's wish, I didn't mean to hurt people," I say. "I don't understand why Linx does it his way. Why does he grant things in the opposite way that people mean?"

"Something happened to him," Uncle Max says. "Long, long ago. It's a story for another time. But remember what I told you earlier, when people tell you their wishes, they're telling you about themselves–the things that make them most vulnerable, the things they most want to change?" I nod. "Well, Linx likes to exploit weaknesses as he grants wishes, turning dreams into nightmares instead of making dreams come true. That's what he was trying to do to you. Turns out–you're stronger than he'd bargained for."

The door to Heddle's office swings open.

"There you are, genie," Trey says. "Bet you thought you could make your escape when I went to the bathroom. I won't be letting you out of my sight again until all my wishes are granted."

"He doesn't remember," I say to Uncle Max. "Is it like a dream to him, too?"

"More like the blink of an eye," Uncle Max says.

"How did he know where to find me?"

"There's some leftover magnetic energy between the two of you. I'm sure he felt his way here without even realizing it."

"Whoa, whoa, whoa," Trey says. I see him take in Uncle Max, who is back to looking like the Uncle Max I've always known–crazy hair and rumpled clothes. "Who the heck is he?"

"You can see him?" I turn to Uncle Max. "He can see you?"

"He has genie vision, for now," Uncle Max explains. "He rubbed your bottle."

"*My* bottle," Trey says, swiping it away from me. I'd managed to hold on to it for a total of about thirty seconds. Trey's eyes flick around the room to Mr. Heddle's desk. "What is going on? Did you put a spell on him?"

"No, he's fine," I say. He doesn't look completely convinced, and I take the opportunity to grab the bottle back and clutch it to my chest tighter than ever.

Trey balls his hands into fists, and for a second I'm afraid he's going to hit me. "My dad is the third-richest man in the United States," he says. "If you don't give my property back to me, he'll hire every lawyer in the entire country to sue you to get it back. Besides which, you're my genie and I'm telling you to give me back the bottle. I'm your master, so you have to obey me."

"We prefer to think of it more like a partnership," Uncle Max tells him. "Less of a genie-and-master situation."

Like I'd pick Trey for my partner. I guess the point is, I don't get to pick who I'm matched with. Which makes him feel like my master after all.

"But he can have the bottle, Zack," Uncle Max says. "Just keep your eyes on it."

Trey smugly takes it back.

"You're welcome," I say.

"You didn't even want to give it to me. I should be thanking . . . whoever the old man is."

"Trey, this is my uncle Max," I say. "Uncle Max, this is Preston Hudson Twendel the third. He goes by Trey." *Or Twerp*, I think to myself.

"Pleased to meet you," Uncle Max says.

"Yeah, you too," Trey says. "Are you a genie, too?"

"As a matter of fact, I am," says Uncle Max.

"I hope you have more experience than this newbie."

"Just a few hundred years," Uncle Max says.

"Excellent, because I haven't gotten any of my wishes yet."

"Think back," Uncle Max tells him. "Before you stepped into the bathroom stall, was there anything you wished for?"

"I just said I didn't get any," he says.

"You wished to be someone other people liked," I tell him. "My sister has a lot of friends, so that's who I turned you into."

"What? I didn't want to be turned into someone else!" Trey says. "I wanted to be me."

"Well, you are again," I tell him.

"Do I have any friends?"

I look at Uncle Max, and he gives a slight shake of his head. "No," I admit.

"So I'm returning that wish. Actually, it's already returned, since I'm me again. And now I demand a new one. And if you don't give me one, I'll sue."

"The court system you speak of doesn't work in our world," Uncle Max tells him.

"But I still have more wishes, don't I?"

Uncle Max shakes his head. "It's one wish per visit, I'm afraid."

"So if you guys go away, and I let some time pass, can I rub the bottle again and get more?"

"The bottle will probably make a nice pencil holder, or a vase," Uncle Max says. "It's not going to be too useful to you once Zack and I leave— and I have a feeling that'll be happening pretty soon."

"But wait!" Trey says. "What's the point of having a genie, then, if everything is going back to the way it was before?"

There's a loud knock at the door—so loud, it sounds menacing. It sounds the way Linx would knock, if he were here. Is he back? Would he knock on the door?

My stomach clenches in fear, and over at the desk, Mr. Heddle is startled awake. "I just had the weirdest dream!" he exclaims to himself. Then he notices other people in the room with him. At least he notices Trey. "Sorry," he says. "I sent for you earlier. I didn't realize you'd arrived."

"What did you dream about?" Trey asks him.

"You know, I can't remember."

The knock sounds again–louder and more room-shaking than before.

"I bet that's your father," Mr. Heddle says.

"My father?"

"Well, of course. We couldn't find you, and he said he was firing up his private jet to find you himself." Mr. Heddle pauses to take a deep breath. "Come in!"

The door bangs open, and in walks a man, his body as thick as a square. He's completely bald and his forehead is as shiny as a mirror. He claps a pair of thick hands together, and it makes a sound like thunder. "Heddle, I demand an update on my son."

"He was just here a second ago."

"I've been calling and calling this office, Heddle. You tell me my son is missing, and then you don't pick up the phone to give me an update. And now you're telling me you've lost him again?"

"Uh, Mr. Twendel," Mr. Heddle stutters. "I, uh . . . I don't know what to tell you."

Trey comes out from his hiding spot behind a ficus plant. "Dad," he says. "I'm here. He found me."

In two huge, swift steps, Preston Hudson Twendel II moves toward his son. I see Trey brace himself for impact, and I brace myself, too. But instead of hurting Trey, his father grabs him in a hug.

"Dad!" Trey says. "Dad. I can't breathe."

Preston Hudson Twendel II loosens his grip

on his son. "I'm sorry about that," he says gruffly.

"I can't believe you're here," Trey says.

"Of course I'm here. The question is, where were you?"

"Well, Dad. It's kind of a long story."

"I canceled my afternoon meeting," Trey's dad says. His thick arms are folded across his chest. "So I have time for a long story."

Trey was right about his dad–he looks powerful, the kind of powerful that people are afraid of. But there's something that makes me feel like things aren't exactly the way they were before. Like right now, the corners of Trey's mouth are turned up just slightly in a smile.

I want to hear the explanation he comes up with for his dad, but I can't listen right now because there's a tingling in my toe. More than a tingling. It feels like it's alive. Like it's about to take flight.

"Uncle Max?" I say.

But Uncle Max is shrinking, in parts, right

before my eyes. Shrunken torso. Shrunken limbs. "I'll see you at home," he says. Then his head shrinks, and he whizzes through the air toward the bottle.

A few seconds later, so do I.

20

Here's What Happens in the End

It is already dark out when I land with a soft thud right back where I started, in Uncle Max's backyard.

You'd think I'd be better at landing, having been through it once before, but this time when I land on the grass, I roll straight into the dirt.

Someone says something, but I can't make it out with my infinitesimally sized ears. The best way I can describe it is to say it's like being underwater, and not being able to understand the words people above the water are saying.

But then: *pop, pop.*

There they are, back to their regular size.

"What?" I ask.

"Watch the flower beds," Uncle Max calls. I look over and there he is sitting on the back porch. His face is lit up, but not in a genie way. It's just because the porch lights are turned on. He's pouring himself a glass of iced tea. I race up the steps, dusting myself for bits of dirt and grass and petals as I go. My heart is pounding like I'm still hurling through tunnels from one side of the bottle to the other.

Uncle Max holds the pitcher out toward me. "Care for a glass?" he asks, like everything is perfectly normal and nothing out of the ordinary happened today. Like my biggest problem is maybe perhaps I'm just a bit thirsty.

"I have to go see Quinn!" I say.

Back down the steps, around the corner, down the block, and up the three steps to our front door. I ring the bell, but I don't wait for anyone to answer. I take the key that Mom hides inside a special rock and bang through the door. "Quinn! Quinn! QUINNNNNNNNNNN!"

Our house isn't that big, but it feels bigger than usual as I race through rooms, not finding her. Not until I trip over her, and fall onto Madeline, sprawled out on the floor in our den.

"OW!" Madeline cries.

"Watch it, nut job," Quinn tells me.

There she is. My sister. I stare at her, taking her in. She looks all right. She looks just like she always does.

"What?" Quinn asks. "Why are you smiling like that?"

"No reason," I tell her. "I was looking for you and now you're here."

"Zack, you're being a nut job," Quinn says. She waves her hand, her signal for *get lost*. "Can't you see we're watching a movie?"

On the TV screen, two girls who don't look much different from Quinn and Madeline are painting each other's nails.

"Stop smiling so much," she says. "It's weird. And do something about your feet."

I look down at my bare feet. I left one shoe at Millings Academy, and the other one at Uncle Max's house. My genie bite looks a little darker than usual. But maybe it's just that the lights are dimmed in the den, better for watching a movie. Can Quinn tell?

"What about my feet?"

"They stink!" she says. "They're stinking up the whole room."

Uncle Max walks in right then. "Well, hello, birthday twins," he says brightly. "And hello, Madeline."

"Hi," Madeline says softly. Then she leans over and whispers something to Quinn. I think I hear the word *Einstein*, which makes both of them laugh. And yes, Quinn's laugh is as cringe-worthy as ever, but neither she nor Madeline seem to care.

"I didn't hear the doorbell ring," I tell Uncle Max.

"The door was unlocked," he says.

"I guess I forgot to lock it behind me," I say.

"Hold the phone," Quinn says. She's looking at me with the same look of disbelief she had when I told her I was a genie. "YOU forgot to lock the door? Don't you know there are a million break-ins a year?"

"Three million," I say. "But I had other things on my mind."

"Oh, look, my whole family is together," Mom says.

Mom is carrying a bowl of popcorn, and she sets it on the coffee table for everyone to share. I don't mention how easy it is to choke on popcorn, or remind everyone to chew an extra amount before they swallow. I just look around at my sister, my uncle, my mom, and even Madeline. All together. "It's great, isn't it?" I say.

"Shh, we're watching the movie," Quinn tells me.

"You talked first," I remind her.

"No, I didn't. Besides, you're talking more."

Mom shakes her head. "I thought maybe the fights would stop when we hit the decade mark."

"Sorry to break up the family scene, but I have to get going," Uncle Max says.

"Can't you stay to the end of the movie?" Mom asks.

"Not this time. I have a bit of work to do." He stands, and Quinn stands, too.

"Can you pause the movie?" she asks. "I have to go to the bathroom. Plus, we should go back a bit because everyone was being so loud."

"Walk me to the door, Zack," Uncle Max tells me.

Standing in our teeny foyer, Uncle Max tells me he plans to write to SFG tonight to tell them I should start in the intermediate class. "If you can tell me what you learned today, Zack."

"I learned you were right about keeping an eye on that bottle," I say. "Except . . ."

"Don't worry, Zack," Uncle Max says to me,

pulling it out of a pocket in his shirt I didn't know was there. "I was watching it for you. Now, did you learn anything else?"

"Well, I've been thinking about the wish Trey made—not the one I ended up granting, but before that. He told me he'd wish to get rid of his dad. And I don't think that's what he really wanted. I think sometimes people wish for things because they want them, and sometimes they wish for things because they're afraid. Like Trey was really afraid of his dad. Mostly, he was afraid his dad didn't like him. That's why he wanted to change."

"That must have been a sad thing for you to see—a son not appreciating his father, and vice versa."

"Yeah, but did you see in the end when his dad showed up? That was his real wish. He didn't even make it, and it came true. He was so afraid of his dad, but in the end it turned out he didn't have to be. So I guess I learned sometimes you have to listen to your fears. And sometimes you have to do the thing you're afraid of, and it'll make you happy."

"And how did that make you feel?"

"It made me happy, too. It was nice that that happened because of me–even if I didn't know I was doing it when I was granting his wish. But that was the best part. It's cool if that's part of my destiny."

"You know, you've reached the final stage of finding out you're a genie," Uncle Max says.

"What's that?"

"Happiness."

"Zack!" Quinn shouts. "You didn't put the toilet seat down!"

"I haven't been home all day!" I shout back.

"Well, who else could it have been, nut job?"

"Quinn, don't call your brother names," Mom says. I smile at Uncle Max. "And, Zack, go put down the toilet seat."

"Go take care of it," Uncle Max says. "And

then get some rest. Tomorrow will be a whole new adventure."

I shut the door behind him, but before I head down the hall, I lift my fist to my chin and say to the imaginary Drew Listerman: "How's that for a day in the life!"

Acknowledgments

Growing up, two of my dearest wishes for adulthood were: (1) to write books, and (2) to be friends with other authors. I want to thank all of my writing pals for helping to make those wishes come true—and thanks especially to Sarah Mlynowski and Laura Schechter, for providing such wonderful spaces for the magic to happen. Thanks also to Gitty Daneshvari, for the dinner conversation that stretched my imagination and changed the course of the story, and to Adele Griffin, for an essential early read.

Thank you to my nephew Zach, the original Zacktastic, and to a few more young friends who read the first draft of this book . . . and then later drafts, and yet more drafts: Avery and Chase, Madden and Brody, and Maverick and Memphis–you guys rock! And thanks to your moms–my stepsister, Laura Liss, and my dear friends Lindsay Aaronson, Amy Bressler, and Logan Levkoff, who fielded all my e-mails and phone calls.

Speaking of phone calls–thank you, Erin Cummings, Jennifer Daly, Regan Hofmann, Arielle Warshall Katz, Geralyn Lucas, Alyssa Sheinmel (my sis!), Elaine Sheinmel (my mom!), Jess Rothenberg, Bianca Turetsky, and Meg Wolitzer, for being on the other end of the phone, all hours of the day.

Thanks to my stepdad, Phil Getter, for loving this story from the very first chapter; to my dad, Joel Sheinmel, for being the world's most willing and enthusiastic proofreader; and to Kai Williams, for her amazing eleventh-hour notes.

Thank you to Laura Dail, Tamar Rydzinski,

and everyone at the Laura Dail Literary Agency, for the ongoing support and cheerleading. (That includes you, Katie Hartman!)

Thank you to the Sleeping Bear Press team for giving Zack Cooley–and while we're at it, Stella Batts–a home. Special thanks to Judy Gitenstein, Heather Hughes, Lois Hume, and Audrey Mitnick. And to my editor, Barb McNally, "thanks" doesn't seem to be enough, but I'll say it anyway: Thank you, Barb, for making *Zacktastic* better than I ever could have on my own.

Finally, my unending gratitude to my entire family for being my family. I love you all so much, you can't even measure it.

ABOUT THE AUTHOR

Courtney Sheinmel is the author of several books for kids and teens, including *Edgewater*, *Sincerely*, and the Stella Batts series. She lives in New York City and hopes you'll visit her online at www.courtneysheinmel.com.